MW01593183

One Good Year

By Larry Gaffney

Level 4 Press, Inc.

Dedication

To my family.

ONE GOOD YEAR

The author of this book is solely responsible for the accuracy of all facts and statements contained in the book. This is a work of fiction. All of the characters and events portrayed in this novel are either fictitious or used fictitiously.

Published by
Level 4 Press, Inc.
13518 Jamul Drive
Jamul, CA 91935
www.level4press.com

BISAC Subject Heading: FIC038000 FICTION / Sports

Library of Congress Control Number: 2006937612

ISBN: 978-1-933769-17-2

Printed in China

ONE GOOD YEAR

The winter was so dreadful that I often felt like Shackleton, huddled and miserable, while Antarctic gales buckled the walls of his tent. Well, my apartment *was* drafty, and sometimes the kid who shoveled the walk didn't show up, so I would be forced to sit in my chair all day wrapped in a blanket, eating cookies out of a box and watching Judge Judy.

Okay, so it wasn't just the winter. It could have been a Parisian spring out there and I still would have been a fat, frowning, chair-filling slug. For reasons that had little to do with the weather, I had fallen into a malaise of self-pity. Exhibit A: my apartment was filthy. Now wait—this was not the kind of filth you see on the evening news, when the authorities have to wear HazMat suits to enter a house filled with fleas, starving pets, and hundreds of gallon jugs filled with the urine of its bewildered occupant, but it was filth all the same. On the kitchen floor, crumpled fast food wrappers and tiny dark things that might be hardened fragments of chocolate icing or morsels of pepper steak, or both. On the countertops, old pizza boxes and cardboard containers sticky with the remains of Chinese takeout. A pile of laundry souring on the rug next to the bathroom door. Dust everywhere, newspapers on the sofa, fly carcasses littering the windowsills (and this was December!). I had lost the impetus to clean, to cook, to pick up after myself. I barely had the energy to step into the shower, and only a lifelong habit of clean-shavenness compelled me to address, once a week or so, the stubble on my cheeks and chin

More than one acquaintance who observed my lifestyle said I was a bum. Bums, I would say, don't live in nice apartments with the cable TV going. True, they would say, but look at you. You're unshaven and your hair is greasy and you're sitting around in your underwear at three in the afternoon. There's dishes in the sink and crap on the floor and roaches, no doubt, napping under the stove. I would defend myself by explaining that since my work was spotty I could shave when I felt like it, and that a little mess gave the place character. Well, they would say, what *about* your work? Substitute teachers shouldn't have a lot of days off in the wintertime, when the regular teachers wake up in the dark and see snow coming down and decide to call in sick.

I don't want to give you the impression that my acquaintances were in the habit of coming over just to cause trouble. They would say these things after they'd been sitting idly for an hour or so, bored with the TV and disappointed that there wasn't any beer in the fridge. They would pick on me and usually I deserved it, for I had become a whiner, giving tongue to my worries. We can solve your problems much better at a bar, they would say, with drinks lubricating the thought process. I would decline and they would leave, and I would be on my own for another night. For solace, and to keep from drinking, I would watch a monster movie while stuffing myself woozy with a take-out dinner.

What stung the most was not having a career. I knew that successful men in their mid-thirties had already put in the hard years of schooling and were well situated as lawyers or doctors or accountants. Not that I ever wanted to be any of those things, but being short on cash and self-respect, I yearned for a well-appointed office, a fat paycheck, and the adoring gaze of a hot secretary. And all I had was my name in a pool of substitute teachers. This gave me enough work to pay the rent and keep the larder stocked and take care of the cable bill, and that was about it.

November and December had been tough, as they are for all lonely, recovering drunks everywhere. Don't ask me how I made it through without going off the wagon. But I did make it, and now it was the end of January, and that's when my old friend Ray Whipple called. He said his marriage had gone bad and asked could he stay with me for a while. I said sure, why the hell not. I told Ray I could use the company, and that we would have a swell time being devil-may-care bachelors around town.

8

Right, he said, we'll have some fun. But there was a catch in his voice that told me his feelings were all torn up. After I got off the phone I had second thoughts. The last thing I needed was a heartsick mope running up my bill with calls to an estranged wife. Such calls, I knew, might last for an hour, and could end with shouting and a hole punched through the wall. But Ray was a buddy, and I had a vacant couch in the living room.

Three days after the call I picked Ray up at the airport and was had by the thumb trick, which is a crude stunt sometimes perpetrated during an embrace between two friends who have not seen each other in a very long time. When we hugged—in a rugged, manly, non-homosexual way, as good friends will do—Ray snuck his hand down into his pocket and activated the pad of his thumb so that it pressed against my leg. I backed away in disgust. "I didn't expect this from a grown-up man over thirty," I said.

"I feel it's important to set the tone early on," said Ray.

That night we went to McDonald's for drive-through. Ray liked the voice of the girl who took our order. I had to admit it was a nice voice even through the wires and plastic of a squawk box. When we pulled around to the window and got a look at her, Ray told me he liked her even better. The girl was pretty and about seventeen, just the type I would ogle in secret while on a subbing job. She had blonde hair tied back and a smile so bright it filled me with the pain of longing. When she held out the brown bags of food, I wanted to caress her pale arms. But I did not act upon this desire, and during the exchange of money I made a point of not getting a finger-feel, because a man has to have some dignity. In the seat beside me, Ray was making the strangled noises an animal might make if it suddenly acquired a taste for beauty, and before I could drive off he made an obscene remark. The remark was obscene only because of its coarse language. The content—that he would brave a sea of excrements for the honor of masturbating in this lovely girl's shadow—was simply intended to inform her of Ray's chivalrous nature. All the same, I wished he had kept silent.

Fortunately, the girl turned back to her register and failed to hear this. On the other hand, maybe she heard it but was too glad with herself to take notice.

For over a year I had been living without much purpose. But at least I had not made things worse by being a drunk. I mention this because for a time I drank heavily and as a result lost a good wife and a succession of decent jobs. What caused me to stop drinking for good was showing up for a job interview one day in my bathrobe and slippers.

It was nine in the morning and I was already drunk, but not so drunk that I didn't know I was finishing myself in the world of business. And it was a fine job they were offering, too, this company that made hanging folders. I was cashing in a reference from an old coach who knew of my troubles. Rumors of the crash-and-burn ending of my previous job had turned me into a figure of fun. At conferences and sales meetings my name would come up during dinner conversation as salesmen traded legends and war stories. The fistfight in a motel parking lot with my sales manager had in fact occurred, but the dismantling of my company car and the shipping of its various parts to locations in three different states was fabrication. On the day of the bathrobe, another legend was born. Skilled tellers of the tale would begin by describing the way the plastic soles of my cheap slippers clacked on the pavement when I got out of the car and entered the Marriott. They would say that I ignored the bellhop and strolled like any respectable businessman down the soft-carpeted corridor in search of the interviewer, stopping to squint at the room number on the folded piece of paper I extracted from the pocket of my navy blue bathrobe. The man in the suit and tie who opened the door had a big smile on his face, but it disappeared pretty fast. He might have thought I was somebody from the room next door—certainly not the guy coming for the interview—but even so he couldn't have liked seeing my chin stubble and uncombed hair. When I said I was there for the job, the man had the presence of mind to step into the hall and close the door. I tried to shake his hand but by then the bellhop was behind me, tugging at my elbow and offering to walk me back out to my car. I babbled a little about my qualifications before giving up and thanking both men for their trouble. I was shaking and on the verge of tears. The bellhop assisted me into the driver's seat and looked like he was thinking about calling the cops. I sped out of the parking lot and ended up in the joint anyway, after ramming into the back end of a *Tastykake* truck. I remember a cascade of packaged pastries upon the windshield, a cursing driver, and then of course the authorities. For days afterward my life was pure shit as I was dragged shamefaced through the system. First, there was the drying out in jail, a county lock-up with Spartan facilities. Then came the fine, the license suspension, and interment at a rehab center, where I was forced to do menial housecleaning chores and had to sit in hard-backed chairs while listening to the rants and sob stories of my fellow addicts.

But I got with the program. I attended a bunch of AA meetings, got my license back, started building my life up to where it had been. I became a substitute teacher for three different school districts, and the work was steady. It was all okay until around Thanksgiving, when I began to feel sad and tired, and stopped looking after myself.

But at least I was no longer a drunk. Not even to be sociable would I allow myself a single glass of beer. Having Ray around would be a challenge, I knew, for the man drank a six-pack a day without thinking about it, and on weekends felt the need to get properly drunk on wine or hard liquor. I could not ask him to become a teetotaler, but when I explained my situation he proved agreeable to a modification of his habits.

"What I'll do," said Ray, "is not ask you if you want a beer every time I go to the fridge and get one for myself."

"That will help," I said.

Ray thought this over for a minute. "Tell you what else I'll do," he said. "I'll pour the beer into a glass. I know if it was me trying to stay on the wagon, I'd rather see a person drinking beer from a glass than from a can. Hell, you might even be able to pretend it's apple juice."

"Sure," I said. "And to complete the illusion, you might consider drinking it with a straw."

Ray had no truck with straws, but he was an all-right guest. He didn't mind bunking in the front room. A sound sleeper, he would lie snoring into the cushions of the sofa, undisturbed by clattering silverware or music from the radio. He lived out of a suitcase, threw his dirty laundry into a green plastic bag, used paper towels to wipe his stray piss off the bathroom tiles. With his wife and young daughter he'd been living in a tract home, a sterile place on a treeless lot. Now, even in his sorrow, he seemed to appreciate the apartment, the ground floor of a subdivided Victorian mansion, with high ceilings and wainscoting and a big bay window in the living room, through which you could see the massive trunk of an ancient oak.

Late February brought a blizzard and an ice storm, and Ray and I were stuck in the apartment—not a good situation. Being off drink had improved my appetite, and now when I stayed up late to watch TV with Ray, I would gorge myself bleary-eyed on shrimp with garlic sauce from The Laughing Buddha, and take in huge roiling banks of Ray's second-hand smoke. Ray had a cold that wouldn't quit and a pot-belly from all the beer he had drunk during the disintegration of his marriage. Still, he worked out every day. A few pushups and leg-lifts on the hardwood floor, and masochistic jogs through the wintry streets, from which he would return red-faced and hacking, with frozen snot droplets on his mustache.

We had become friends while playing football at Rexford, a small college in Upstate New York. Ray was good, a scatback with the rabbit-like instincts of a moving thing that fears capture. He won recognition and even had a shot with the Jets. But at five-seven, one-eighty, he was considered too small for the pros.

Me, I was not a stand-out college player. I'm good at catching the ball, but I have very small hands. I'm fairly quick, and I'm football-smart, with a sense of how to find open space on the field. But I lack foot-speed, so at Rexford most of the passes were thrown to Verdan Fraley, a sprinter with hands like giant spiders. A girlfriend once made fun of my hands, calling them "little raccoon paws," and saying they were best suited for furtive things like a fast nose-pick when no one was looking.

A girlfriend was something I could have used that winter. At one of the high schools there was a Spanish teacher, a divorced, fortyish, plump lady with a pretty face and large bosoms who seemed interested in me. She had a smart mouth on her, and we would spar in the faculty room during morning coffee. But I heard stories of a stalking ex-husband, a teenage daughter with a flair for melodrama, upheavals coming all of a sudden, and so I made no move.

Sometimes I would flirt with a short, perky counter-girl at Dunkin Donuts. I consider short girls sexy, especially if they have blonde hair, like this donut girl. I like tall girls, too, but tend to think of them as potential life-partners who will look out at the world from a height comparable to my own. This may be a stupid prejudice, but I like it that a short girl's vision is easily focused on my chest, my midsection, my groin. Her little legs can wrap around me and I can get up and carry her to some other part of the room without coming unstuck. Also, a short girl can dance naked on a chair without tipping it over.

Such things I would imagine while chomping a jelly donut and sipping milk. The girl would lean forward with her arms on the counter, a dusting of powdered sugar on her knuckles, teasing me with small talk. But somehow I couldn't make a move on her, either.

I wasn't afraid of rejection, that, I can tell you for sure. "Get lost, creep," or words of that type I have heard many times in my search for available women, a search I regard as the proper activity of every man who has not fallen prey to an early marriage or some religion that puts the hurt on natural desire. I know that the brush-off is part of the deal, that you have to annoy ten women to score with one.

But I had a sense that things weren't right with me, that I was standing water and shouldn't pull anyone in. I was still smarting from being divorced by a woman I had truly loved, and I wasn't eager to start up anything new. And I had trouble thinking of myself as any kind of a catch, what with not having a real job or any prospects. Staying up late watching TV with Ray had already cost me a few subbing jobs. They would call at six in the morning, which was often only a couple of hours since I'd rolled into bed.

Neither one of us got laid that winter. Ray would go for days without calling Barbara, but then he'd pick up the phone and make the damn call. I would come into the room and Ray would already have his voice up, pacing with the cordless phone clenched to his ear. When this happened I always went out for groceries or a paper. Later he'd suggest we have a night on the town and bring some girls back to the apartment, but it never happened.

Ray would ask me, "How do we do that with you not drinking? No woman will give you a second look when you're at the bar nursing a sodey-pop."

I would argue that times had changed, that there were plenty of guys on the wagon and women knew that and respected it. Ray would take up the argument and we would decide to continue it over a delivered pizza, and then TV would again occupy our full attention.

The first week in April, when I was practically in despair over what to do, I received a call from Lou Levine. I had known Lou for years, ever since he hired me one summer to work at Catawba, an athletic camp for boys where he was the director. Lou was short and wiry, with the intense aspect of the born coach and teacher. An hour after I'd met him for the first time he was telling me what I should do to get my life in order, and I was buying it.

Lou enjoyed confrontations. Once when he was a college coach and his team had traveled to my city for a game, I paid him a visit in his hotel room. By the closet door sat a pair of shoes—pointy-toed, two repulsive colors (cadaver gray and excremental brown), and tassels, which I find ignoble. I understood that Lou was sharing the room with the team's trainer, who might very well be the owner of the shoes, but I also knew he was prone to grave sartorial misjudgments.

"Those your shoes?" I asked.

Lou stopped what he was doing, turned from the duffel bag on the bed, and faced me square on, like he was ready to fight. "Yeah, those are my shoes. Why? You got a problem?"

"No problem at all," I said. "I was just wondering if they were yours or the other guy's."

"You don't like the shoes?" The way Lou said it, he might have been asking if I'd raped his sister.

I shrugged. "So they're the Quasimodo of shoes, who cares." What disturbs me is that you're so defensive. You seem tense, uptight. Is there something wrong in your life, Lou? What the hell's going on?"

A beatific smile settled upon Lou's face. "My life has never been better. But I wonder about the mentality of a man who walks into a room and starts asking questions about a pair of shoes."

Before I could answer, the trainer came in and almost tripped over the shoes. "Keep those ugly fuckin' shoes outa my way," he said, and that was the end of that.

Now, when I heard Lou's crisp, New York-accented voice, I hoped for good news. Lou was feisty and sometimes difficult, but he had a deep commitment to helping his friends.

"Are you in shape?" he asked.

I hesitated. "Been in worse."

"Okay," said Lou, "so you're a fat fuck. That we can remedy. What else are you doing? I mean besides feeding your face. Are you working?"

"For the record," I said, "I'm not really fat. Maybe a bit flabby around the middle. Of course I'm working. Just not every day. I happen to be a substitute teacher. Actually, I'm thinking about graduate school."

He ignored the lie about graduate school. "Forget the subbing. I have something you might be interested in."

"I don't know," I said. "If it's another camp job..."

"It isn't. Now put away your dick and turn off *I Dream of Genie*. This is a good deal."

And so it was. Lou had been named head coach of a team in the Northeast Football Association, a start-up league with solid investors and high hopes. The cities were second-tier and the geographical area limited, but ESPN had already signed on to cover the games. The NFA had a decent chance of making it. Even the newspapers were saying so.

Lou needed a man to coach the receivers and maybe fill in as a player now and then. Did I want the job?

I considered my options. Dwindling funds. The physiologic perils of late sleeping and lying about. The lug inhabiting my sofa.

"When do I report?" I asked.

The set-up was not so bad. I knew from experience how cheesy it could get with a low-rent sports franchise, having played a season with a semi-pro team out west. Back then we had practices in a public park. We had to rely on our own beat-up vehicles because a team bus was out of the question. One time the fullback's car wouldn't start. Since all the players had left for the game, there was no one he could call for a ride. (He was a man plagued by personal demons; his friends had given up on him and his neighbors would yell that they were dialing 911 if he even approached their doorstep.) He lived beyond the range of public transport, so he hitch-hiked, in full uniform, and made it with only a few minutes gone in the second quarter.

But this was a different situation altogether. I could see by the facilities that some money was available. Teddy Mankopf, the mortuary tycoon, had bought a dying prep school and run everyone off the place. It was at the city's edge with big shade trees all around. The buildings were ivy-covered stone and brick. There was an old football stadium, and Mr. Mankopf had renovated it with funds earned by his very successful chain of discount funeral parlors. A high-class locker room had been added on, with a separate wing full of gleaming chromium weights, floor-to-ceiling mirrors, and pneumatic torture machines for the building of muscle tissue. Best of all, team members could live rent-free in the vacant dormitories, sparing us the dismal affair of apartment hunting.

We were the Centerport Cossacks and we had a terrific logo: a bearded warrior with blazing red eyes—wearing black boots and a Cossack hat, of course—on a rearing stallion, scimitar held high for lopping off heads and limbs. But the word Cossacks could lend itself to obscene permutations. I foresaw that opposing fans would call us cocksacks. So I suggested to Lou that the team name be changed to Hessians.

"We'd have pretty much the same logo," I said, "and you can't twist Hessians into any dirty words that I can think of."

Lou shook his head. "I doubt Mr. Mankopf would want anyone confusing him with Leon Hess."

I saw the point immediately. In case you're not a follower of pro football, Leon Hess was the famous owner of the New York

Jets before he died. I could understand Mr. Mankopf wanting to keep his identity clear, since he was the one footing the bill.

"Anyway," continued Lou, "the logo would have to be a little different. Hessians were German, they didn't wear those big hats. This town is loaded with boonyaks from Eastern Europe. Their brains are more likely to resonate to the word Cossacks."

After a few days driving around town checking out the inhabitants, I began to recognize the Slavic type Lou was talking about. A burly or sinewy guy—in any case, tough looking—with a brush cut and a potato nose, giving me the hard stare from his obsessively manicured front lawn.

If that sounds negative about Slavic people I'm sorry, but I've never understood why everybody resents being reduced to a stereotype. Hell, stereotypes make sense to me. As a full-blooded Irishman named Finbar Connors, I know that a lot of the stuff said about micks is dead-on, because I've seen evidence of it in my own family. My grandfather Liam used to say that if the Connors clan had a coat of arms, it would be a drunkard fumbling with his tie to get ready for Sunday mass. It was a point of pride with him that no Connors man ever went to church with a hangover—they were all still drunk from the night before. My grandmother Helen put up with such talk because that's what Irish women of her generation did. But putting up for years with her drunken husband, his drunken brothers and their drunken friends, while raising seven children on a house-painter's wage, had turned her sour and mean-spirited. Once when I was a kid I sat with her on a crowded beach. She wore an old-fashioned black bathing suit, and her eyes were shaded by a black, wide-brimmed hat. From somewhere close by came a woman's robust, throaty laughter. On and on it went, some broad having a terrific time for herself. "She must be fat," said my grand-mother.

Slavs or Irish or anything else, it didn't matter to me so long as they filled the seats.

Life was good. I was drawing a paycheck and I had a place to stay and interesting work to do. By pulling strings with Lou I managed to get a tryout for Ray Whipple. He performed well and they gave him a contract. I wouldn't have minded rooming with him again but as an assistant coach I had the option to have a room of my own, and I went for it. I like a little solitude now and then.

My days were full of meetings and practice and workouts. I did plenty of sprinting and weight-lifting, and at the end of the day, after a bracing dinner in the old refectory, I would stroll along the quiet, shaded walkway back to my room, enjoying the medley of whirrs and clicks from insects hiding in the pale weeds. Then I would spend an hour on my bed, empty-headed, drowsy, feeling the animal happiness of a full belly and pure inaction. I would mark the slow departure of light from the room, while the murmur of distant traffic rose and fell like the quiet breathing of the world itself.

My teammates might be up to something later on, but I seldom had any interest. I had brought with me a backpack full of books— military history, Zen, sci-fi adventures, a biography of Jack Kerouac. I would lose myself in other worlds, other lives. It would keep me out of trouble.

By the first week in August I was in outstanding physical condition and eager for the start of the season. NFL training camps were already under way. The Cossacks would begin theirs in another week, by which time all of the players would have trickled in. I was excited, but filled with anxiety.

I was, after all, thirty-five, with no profession to turn to after this last try at football. I hoped that a good year might get me noticed and lead to a coaching job at a small college, or perhaps in the NFL. But my resume was weak, and if the NFA folded after its first season, then what would I do? I was too old for law school, or some fool graduate program, or any other kind of training in...what? I began to think of failure as a materializing presence, a demonic bully that might grab the frayed lapels of my jacket and give me the shaking of my life, and I'd never be the same again. Such fear is the best preventative to slacking off. So I centered my mind and paid close attention to the business at hand. I knew it was required.

And I knew something else. I needed a woman.

This became clear to me one Thursday morning at Denny's. I was sitting with Sal Gargano, the defensive coordinator, and two other players, Chunky Hanrahan and DeCurtis Johnson. Coach Gargano had finished off his pancakes and was talking about an author named Ouspensky who'd written a book called *The Psychology of Man's Possible Evolution,* in which, among other things, it is suggested that there is no predestination, that we can choose grandly at a generous buffet of futures. It was an interesting topic, and Coach had the steady, confident delivery of a professor who really knows his stuff. But when he started to bring UFOs and werewolves and such into the picture, as he often did, my mind wandered. DeCurtis was all ears, and Chunky Hanrahan nodded politely while consuming his second order of French toast and bacon.

It was after ten, and the crowd at Denny's was sparse. A sloppy-fat, balding salesman sat alone in a corner booth, dawdling over a plate of pushed-around ham and eggs, seeing dim prospects in the mangled remains of his breakfast. Next to the salesman, a pair of white-haired old ladies quietly dissected their

29

omelets. And across the aisle a skinny, small-faced girl with a dust mop of curly black hair sat munching toast and scanning a copy of USA Today. My gaze traveled the long length of her, top to bottom, and I noticed that she was rubbing the sole of one panty-hosed foot on the serrated crown of her black leather, low-heeled shoe. It pleased me to see that her toenails were painted bright purple, and that her foot was pretty, not narrow and long-toed, as one might expect to see at the end of a tall, skinny girl's ankle. I wished then that I were younger and crazier, so I could slip out of the booth and crabwalk across the aisle and take hold of the girl's foot and plant a sudden kiss on her big toe. I fantasized that my erotic handling of her foot would cause her to lose track of her toast and reading material. Within seconds the girl would have her hose crumpled around her ankles and her skirt raised and we would be copulating on the greasy table to the whistles and exhortations of my comrades. Or, I thought, she might kick viciously at my face and scream for the manager. Both possible futures popped into nothingness as a waitress appeared with the check, and Coach

Gargano concluded his lecture by saying, "Yep, this universe is one helluva strange place."

Since I had a couple of hours to kill before my next meeting, I hurried back to my room and enjoyed a leisurely dissolution while recalling the image of the girl from Denny's. But upon completion I suffered an attack of what Lou Levine calls PMS—Post Masturbatory Sorrow—and decided it was time to get back in the hunt.

It was five years since I'd lost my wife, and I still thought about her almost every day. I had enjoyed many aspects of marriage—I considered myself the marrying type, in fact—and I sorely missed the comforts of domestic life. For most of the marriage Annette and I had been inseparable. Every time I laid eyes on her—whether she was posing seductively in an ensemble from Victoria's Secret, or standing at the sink with her hands in dishwater and loose strands of her chestnut hair plastered to her sweaty forehead—I knew that she was all I would ever want.

Let me say that I do not consider myself the handsomest guy in the world, or perhaps

31

even on the block. Once while talking to a blind date on the phone, I described my looks as falling smack in the middle of a spectrum that had Tyrone Power at one end, and Rondo "The Creeper" Hatton at the other. But the girl wasn't up on her film references—especially the old black and white films of the forties—and was able to wrap her mind only around the name Tyrone. "Are you trying to tell me you have negro blood?" she asked. All that aside, I've always figured I'm *reasonably* good-looking. No girlfriend has ever dumped me because of my face, as far as I know. But Annette was so beautiful that I sometimes felt ill at ease by her side. Her lustrous hair hung down to her shoulders, and she had the face and smile of a cover girl and vivid green eyes. She was curvy but not plump, and the perfection of her legs, I used to tell her, would have been a liability had she lived in ancient Greece, for surely some envious hag on Olympus would have blighted those legs with fire or a disfiguring disease.

When I first met her she seemed always aloof, or distracted. We had a class together in my senior year—*Dimensions of Literature*, they called it. I would appear in gym shorts

32

and a tank top, showing off my tanned muscular limbs as I paraded to my seat. But she never seemed to notice me, except for the few times I asked her some trivial, direct question. She was the kind of person who concentrates on one thing at a time. The poetry being discussed. A question thrown to the class by the fat, seedy professor. Her own lofty thoughts, whatever they were.

I finally got her attention one day at The Oasis, a burger and fries hangout near the campus. She was alone, reading a book and ignoring the small portion of cheeseburger left on her plate. I figured what the hell, and made my move.

"Hi," I said. "You gonna eat the rest of that cheeseburger?"

Annette looked up at me with a disbelieving smile. I guess she figured this was the stupidest pick-up line she'd ever heard, or I was a moron who trolled restaurants to glom the leftovers on people's plates. "Take it away," she said.

I snagged the piece of cheeseburger with my thumb and forefinger and wrapped it in a napkin. Annette watched me do this, her smile fading. She was about to return to her book when I played my card. "It's not for me," I said. "It's for a stray cat I've been feeding."

Now this was absolutely true. I'm a sucker for homeless animals. But I'll be the first to admit that I was using my kind-heartedness to impress her. I figured she'd take the bait, because on a couple of occasions in class she had proved very outspoken on the subject of animal rights.

Annette did not disappoint me. Where was the cat? she wanted to know. Had I checked the classifieds? Maybe someone was looking for it. Oh, she was full of concern, and soon we were at my apartment, slicing the burger into bite-size portions and putting it on a paper plate to take out to the back alley. My roommate at the time was a pie-faced, boorish linebacker who liked dogs, because they obeyed, and hated cats, because they didn't. He would razz me for bothering to feed the mangy thing. But after he got a look at Annette he was all of a sudden St. Francis of Assisi. He offered to donate some steak shavings he had put aside for the building of a late night sandwich, and suggested we also put out a saucer of milk. But lust made me ruthless. I reminded the jerk that just the other day he had thrown an empty beer bottle at the cat when it tried coming up the back steps for the first time. That detail was the only thing Annette would remember about him, especially after we became lovers and stayed always at her apartment, which she had all to herself on a quiet, tree-lined street away from the jock houses and frat houses.

I proposed to her six months after I met her, and to the annoyance of her snooty, old-moneyed Vermont family, she said yes.

It was only after the divorce that I came to appreciate the true meaning of the word "haunted." At times I felt like a ghost dragging a spectral chain of memories down a dark corridor. The happy memories hurt the most because they reminded me of what I'd lost. I kept thinking of our trip to Maine, for example. For months after Annette had left me, retreating to her family home in the Northeast Kingdom and contacting me only through an attorney, I could not for the life of me shake the vivid recollection of that trip. It had been early in the marriage, when I had a sales job that took me all over New England,

and since I was not under close supervision I often brought Annette with me. I would station her in a motel room where she would happily spend the day napping and reading and gabbing with her sister on the phone. I would return after making my sales calls and take her sight seeing and out for a fine meal on the company expense account. On the trip to Maine, Annette wanted to spend at least one night sleeping under the stars, so I found a campground overlooking the sea. It was October and the nights were chilly, and the wind came up just after we'd zipped our sleeping bags together. There was wood smoke in the air and fallen leaves scuttering all around us. We lay side by side on a mossy patch, looking up at the night sky where the wind shivered the stars. We made love gently, and afterward listened to the distant clanging of a buoy.

The next day we stopped at a tourist shop converted from an old barn. It sold everything from hard candy to lobster traps, and I bought her a set of wind chimes made of miniature buoys. I told her that even though we didn't have a porch to hang them on, I hoped someday we would, and her eyes got misty.

Reflecting on such moments caused me no end of suffering. I had always thought of myself as having inner strength, figured I would be all man if it came to a breakup. I never expected to collapse in a chair and begin weeping just because there was no one to greet me with a hug when I came home from work. I had known other poor souls who wasted hours writing "I want you back" letters, or showed up on an ex's doorstep with flowers, only to be turned away, but if anyone had said that would be me, I'd have suggested we take it outside.

I'd have to say that two things helped me get over this awful time in my life. First, Annette remarried—an investment counselor, an older man, as I understand it. So there went any secret hope I might have been holding onto that she would come running back into my arms and my bed. Second, I started reading books on Zen. I wouldn't say that I was any kind of a real student. I had no plans to shave my head and join a monastery. But I read deeply and set my mind to an understanding of basic principles. I liked

Zen's bottom-line message that nothing is real except the moment right there in front of you. I wanted the past to go away and leave me alone. I didn't like the future, either, which had a face—my own, haggard, broken by the sorrows of life, grimacing back at me from the mirror. So yeah, I figured, give me the moment and nothing else. To be in the present you had to meditate, so I learned how to do that. It wasn't easy. The mind, say the Hindus, is a drunken monkey, and mine was a whole troupe of them fighting over the remote. But I concentrated and after a while I got pretty good at it. This prevented me from doing something stupid, like driving up to Vermont in a grand but hopeless attempt at reconciliation. I kept my sanity.

Unfortunately, drinking trumped meditation, and that's when the real trouble started. But now, as a Cossack, I was physically well and had my mind right. I intended to make meditation part of my new life. Alas, the first time I tried to meditate at training camp I forgot to lock my door. Just as I was easing into an altered state, there was a terrible commotion in the hall. The door flew open and Guy Smeeks and Reg Hastings tumbled into my room. Ice cream cones had been served with dinner, and during the walk back to the dorm these two had undertaken to crush and smear the cones and the ice cream into each other's faces. A party of raucous onlookers cheered them from the hallway. Then the boys rolled out of the room and were gone. But the spell had been broken. My hands were even trembling a little.

Maybe I *did* need to be in a monastery. I had read about Zen masters who whacked their students upside the head to make them more aware of the moment. It occurred to me that perhaps the nuns of my Catholic boyhood had been acting in the same spirit when they brought their metal rulers down hard on my knuckles. I was inclined to think otherwise, but would have given any person in authority the benefit of the doubt in order to receive a mild thrashing that might knock thoughts of the past out of my brain.

I was in Lou Levine's office when Coy Jessup came in looking for a job. Jessup was 6'7", 295. After a troubled career at Mississippi State, he'd been on the roster of the Miami Dolphins for a year. The story on Jessup was this: he had unlimited potential but there were bats in his belfry. Prone to violent actions and possessed of the frightening strength imbued in the truly mad, he was a player born to the role of defensive lineman. Coaches and teammates praised his efforts on the playing field, but shied away from him in regular life. The legend of Coy Jessup had been born on the day in his junior year when he threw an assistant coach's chair through a closed door—with the coach still in it.

Now Coy stood in front of Lou's desk, slightly hunched and holding his Nike cap in his hands. "Most of what they say about me just isn't true," he began. "For example, I never ate a live puppy." He went on at some length about anger management and other issues, while Lou listened politely, pursing his lips and nodding his head at appropriate moments.

I could imagine what Lou was thinking. Coy Jessup was loony toons, but our front four needed help. The only man with any real experience was George "Taters" Delevan, an iffy prospect at best. After college, Taters had knocked around the NFL and the Canadian League for a few years as a 240-pound fullback, until his weight ballooned to 285 and he was switched to defensive tackle. Delevan had grown fat because of his passion for the potato in all of its culinary manifestations. He was a man who ate potato chips not by the bag, but by the tin. It was said of Taters Delevan that he could eat more French fries at one sitting than a Boy Scout troop. In Calgary they still told of the time he caught a screen pass on his own 20, bowled over a linebacker, and started up field with nothing but daylight ahead. The only man after him was Virgil Plews, an aging safety who'd once played for the Dallas Cowboys but now spent his off hours in heavy drinking. Plews, suffering on this day from an especially bad hangover, was content to give half-hearted chase and watch Delevan's rumbling hindquarters all the way to the end zone. But just five yards shy of midfield, Delevan slowed to a trot. As he crossed the fifty-yard line he knew he was out of gas, that there would be no more running until he could have a decent rest. Well, he would be the first man ever to *walk* half the field for a touchdown, and he believed this to be a possibility until he heard the rasping breath of Plews at his neck, and felt the jarring tackle that popped the ball from his grasp. Split end Joe McPhee had correctly assumed that Delevan would not be able to run eighty yards, and so was trailing in hope of a lateral. He scooped up the ball on the forty-three and ran it in for a touchdown. It was the winning score, and in the giddy aftermath Delevan's teammates traded tales of the trencherman's heroics some hours before the game at a steakhouse buffet, where he had reportedly consumed nine butter-soaked, chive-sprinkled baked potatoes.

Lou was probably thinking what it would mean to have such a man as Taters Delevan anchoring his defensive line. Then he gazed at the specimen standing before him, possibly insane but strong as a tree. "Okay, Jessup," he said. "You're hired."

Whenever I step on the practice field, I remember all over again why I love the game of football. Part of it is being on grass under a blue sky, or even under a dull gray sky with rain or snow coming down; it really doesn't matter. It's the fun of catching a pass and sidestepping a tackler, making him grab air instead of your jersey. It's hanging with forty or so other guys united by the desire to move fast and hit each other and yell. It's learning and perfecting the splendid skills of the professional football player. It has always pleased me that the skills of my position, wide receiver, are refined and graceful, encompassing avoidance, misdirection, guile, and the paradox of both tensing and softening your hands at the same time for the purpose of gathering in a spiraling football. I have always been glad not to be a large-bodied offensive tackle, forced to learn other skills, like setting your feet so as not to be bowled over, and keeping your body balanced at different angles depending on what play has been called, and becoming inured to the foul breath and flying snot that a typical defensive end will spew forth in his frenzy to attack the ball carrier. At practice I have felt the camaraderie of men who share the pride of mastering positional skills, and who are sustained by this pride when aching and sweat-soaked and badly shaken because an assistant coach has screamed in their faces that they are nothing more than piles of dog puke.

Now the summer sky was filled with racing clouds left over from an early morning thunderstorm, and a cool breeze fluttered our practice jerseys. The field was freshly cut, the yard lines blinding white. All the Cossacks gathered in front of the bleachers to hear Lou Levine address the team as a unit for the first time. Owing to his height of 5' 8", Lou stood on the third bench up so everyone could see him. He wore a Cossacks T-shirt, light green with gold piping. His weathered face was tan and squinty, and the wind ruffled his graying hair. He held in his hand a clipboard with a pen tied to it, and around his leathery neck hung a whistle that many believed he never took off, not even while having sexual intercourse with his wife.

"Men," he said, "you are here to achieve a threefold purpose. First, to individually fulfill your promise as human beings and football players. Yes, that's right, you *are* human beings, regardless of what you've been told all your lives by coaches and educators who have compared you to wombats and tapeworms and other subhuman entities. But you *define* your humanity by playing football, which is the only thing some of you will ever be able to do proficiently, let's face it. Second, you are here to bring that fulfilled promise together as a team. And what is a team? It's a group of men held together by a common goal. That goal is the glue that keeps you working like a dog even though the man next to you might be an alcoholic wife-beating pornocating scumbag. It doesn't matter—he's your teammate. And you and he and everyone else on the team, regardless of race, creed, or sexual orientation, will rip out the entrails of anyone who stands in the way of your shared goal, and that goal is reason number three why you are here, and that reason is to *win*. Winning puts the fire of ecstasy in your heart. Winning is when you take the fat kid's lunch money, when you secretly have deranged animalistic sex with your best friend's fiancé, when you score the fourth-quarter touchdown that puts the big game on ice. Remember how that felt? Ladies, you must have the determination to win at all costs. You must do whatever it takes to win, even if, to paraphrase a great fighter, you are compelled to devour the testicles of your own son."

He paused, lasering his eyes across the line of eager faces before him. Then he shouted, *"Now let's go play some football!"*

Coach Gargano blew his whistle long and hard, and the Cossacks, roaring like men rushing into battle, ran to their stations.

As positional coach of the wide receivers, I took stock of the men under me. The stand-out was Darvis Childs. Though not very big at 5'11", 180, he had blazing speed and ran his routes with confidence and precision. At McNeese State he'd been ignored by NFL scouts because of his reputation as a wideout who dropped too many balls. But now when I lobbed passes in his general direction, Childs caught everything. He would be the go-to guy. The other starter was Placebo Washington, rangy and raw, a junior college dropout Lou had signed after a chance encounter.

Back in June, Lou and I had been working out a couple of hopefuls at defensive back. I ran a few simple routes, and Lou, who'd been a scrambling All-Ivy-League quarterback at Dartmouth, threw tight spirals at me. The two hopefuls weren't doing a very good job covering. But defensive backs coach

Tom Patterson thought they had potential, so the drill went on.

Patterson called for a break so he could lecture the men, and I noticed a tall black kid watching from the sidelines. Shirtless, the kid looked like one of those warriors you'd see on the cover of a comic book, abs and lats standing out like cobblestones. All he needed was a shield and a sword. He had wide shoulders and looked to be about 6' 4", with long arms and no discernable body fat. After a while he sauntered over to where we were standing.

"Mind if I play with y'all?"

Lou looked him up and down. "You want to try covering this old slow white guy?" he said, nodding in my direction.

The kid smiled, showing perfect white teeth. "If it's all the same, I'd rather go out."

Tom Patterson stopped lecturing the hopefuls and frowned at the kid. He was conducting business, after all, and who was this newcomer? The kid wore cut-off jeans and decrepit work boots, and his hands were dusty from the bag of quicklime he'd left on the sidelines. But Patterson kept quiet; Lou was the boss.

"You with the maintenance crew?" asked Lou.

"Tha's right."

"You've played some ball?"

"Here and there."

"You know how to run a down and out?"

The kid's smile got bigger. "Watch me."

He took off his work boots and his dirty white socks. He wiped his hands on the grass and stood poised on the line of scrimmage. Patterson positioned the two defenders. At a signal from Lou, the kid took off. The first defender came up immediately for a bump, but it had no effect; he flew backwards as if he'd collided with a steel pillar. The kid threw a nonchalant fake at the second guy and sped down the field. The defender wasn't much of a cover man, but he had good speed and ran stride for stride with the kid. Lou lofted a pass high into the air, and the kid hit another gear and separated from the defender. It's a beautiful thing to see when the god-given gift of raw speed shows itself all of a sudden, when an athlete breaks away from the pack with the power of a jet tearing across the sky. I watched in awe, waiting for the ball to drop into the kid's outstretched hands. But Lou had misjudged his speed, and the pass was spiraling down short of the mark. The defender kept his stride and brought his hands up for the interception. And then, elegantly, the kid cut his speed, and leapt up and backwards into the air, and with one gigantic hand plucked the ball from its downward trajectory and the reaching arms of the defender. The defender clawed at the kid in frustration, but he was already gone.

That was Placebo Washington. They gave him a few more patterns to run. He got open every time and didn't drop a single ball. Then Patterson covered him, or tried to, with the same result.

Placebo Washington had the talent to play in the NFL, but in his youth, first as a high school star in Coburn, Georgia, and then as a freshman for Western Carolina, he'd been distracted by his hobbies: women, cocaine, and handguns. After some jail time and re-hab, he moved in with an aunt who lived up in Michigan, and played for a year at a junior college there before falling into the same self-destructive patterns. Now, by sheer coinci-dence, he was living with an uncle in Centerport, and working on Mr. Mankopf's maintenance crew. Lou was nervous about the kid's dubious background but offered him a contract anyway. "Everybody needs a third or fourth chance," he said. "Just ask my wife."

The receiving corps was rounded out by James Veltry, Ipana Brown, and myself, who would coach more than play. Veltry, a twenty-eight-year-old veteran of the Canadian Football League, had been cut by the Hamilton Tiger Cats after busting up his knee. But an operation had repaired the damage and he still moved gracefully and fast. He was soft-spoken and handsome, with curly hair and a thin mustache, and rumor had it he was light in the loafers. A confirmed bachelor, as they say. Ipana Brown was an unheralded but competent backup from Cortland State, a small college not far from Centerport. And then there was Fin Connors, thirty-five but in excellent condition, cagey and sneaky-quick and able to come into the game and dive for a low spiral on third and three, and then crawl forward seven inches for the first down before being smashed into the turf.

The starting tight end was Szandor Berenyi, a Hungarian who'd been a soccer goalie at MIT. Two years ago, when Lou was still running his athletic camp, he'd hired Berenyi as a counselor and soccer coach. Berenyi, an amiable type with a hearty laugh, a big, squarish head and a caterpillar mustache, took a liking to American football at the camp, which had on its staff a number of college players. He joined them in their casual workouts, and was impressive at catching passes with his big soccer-goalie hands. One moonlit night, when the campers were snug in their urine-stained bunks, some of the counselors had a drunken, impromptu game of tackle football, and Berenyi, 6' 5" and 240, proved a hard man to bring down. The tumult of this game, played on a field not far from the main lodge, brought Lou out in his boxers and flip-flops, irritated that the noise had shattered the consummation of an erotic dream he was having about a young Jacqueline Bisset, a phantasm he regularly invoked by employing the principles of lucid dreaming, especially during work-related separations from his wife. Lou was all set to yell when he saw Berenyi slogging across the field with a burly counselor attached to one of his legs. Someone else caught up with Berenyi and jumped on his shoulders, riding him like a troll in a fairy tale. The extra weight caused Berenyi to bend low, but still he surged forward. Finally everyone was on him and he collapsed under the heap of laughing, hooting drunkards that Lou later said looked like Morlocks in the moonlight.

The backup tight end was Kenny Liebowitz, a garrulous man with poor speed, average quickness, and questionable hands. At 6'1, 210, he wasn't very big for the position, either. But during his four years at Hofstra and his one season with Barcelona in the European League, he'd managed to do everything asked of him. He had the knack. Typically, a pass would bounce off his hands and somehow wedge between his helmet and the crook of his elbow for a completion. After Lou hired him, he said, "I bet it's good to have a Jew on the team, right?" All these brothers and goyim, you need another Jew around. Am I on target, Coach?"

"Like an Israeli sniper," said Lou.

Liebowitz had new age interests that made some of his teammates smile and shake their heads. The animal cruelty he'd witnessed in Spain, and especially while traveling through the Orient, had put him off meat, and he was now a full-fledged vegan. "Another year or two, I'm off to California to study some kind of alternative medicine, something holistic," he told me. "My first choice was massage therapy, but I found out you can't have a practice where you only do chicks. How fuckin' unjust is that?"

It was a hot August and an even hotter September. Ninety-four and humid on Labor Day. It toughened us. By mid-September we were a crackerjack unit. That's what Sal Gargano called us after an especially crisp practice. "Crackerjack!" he yelled out across the field. "You guys are a crackerjack unit!" And for days afterward he took a ribbing for it. Even Bobby Hertzig, our campy, openly gay cornerback got into the act. "Hey, Coach," he said, waving a hand toward the linebackers and defensive linemen in front of him, "if these guys are crackerjacks, can I be fiddle-faddle?"

In the interest of togetherness, it was requested one day that I accompany the large group of players who regularly went out for beers after dinner. My commitment to sobriety was ignored like the whimper of a child being dragged to the dentist.

"You're coming with us," said Ray Whipple. "You spend every night in your room reading like some egghead. We're afraid it's making you soft. We may lose respect for you. You're coming."

Paul Facemeyer and Klaus Kohler, whose combined weight equaled that of a bedroom set, stood behind Ray, glowering.

"You will drink," said Kohler. "If you are a man."

"That's another issue," said Ray, boring into me with his olive-black eyes. "Some of the guys are beginning to think maybe you're a fag. I know you've had a rough time, but come on, dude, it's been a couple of years. Look at me. I admit I'm still fucked up over Barbara, but does that stop me from getting a blow job when it's available?"

It was true. A week earlier, Ray had enjoyed the oral favors of a barmaid in the back seat of his parked car. The experience had eased a lot of tension from his life.

And Ray was right, I had to admit. I was gun shy because of a doomed relationship I'd started up a few months after my divorce. Her name was Misty, a big-titted brunette with a squarish jaw and a wry grin. She was aggressive and outspoken, attractive qualities in a woman I hoped to seduce on the night of our first meeting. And I had not been disappointed. After an hour or so of sizing each other up in a smoke-filled, noisy bar, we went to my apartment and jumped into bed. Simple as that. We had good chemistry from the start. She came like gangbusters even though I was rather quick on the trigger, a defect owing to my not having been with a woman for some time. Afterward, quite pleased with myself, I just lay there mute and grinning and paralyzed. Dimly, I considered that when I recovered the power of movement I would get up and make a sandwich. Meanwhile Misty was talking non-stop, about what I have no recollection. But I heard her clearly when she said I should turn over so she could massage my back. When that was done she got up to use the bathroom, and when she returned it was after a detour to the kitchen. She had a bag of chips and a plate with some cheese and slices of ham on it. "Hope you don't mind," she said. "I made myself right at home."

I didn't mind a bit. We ate the ham and cheese and some of the chips and watched the tiny TV on a dresser at the foot of the bed. Misty was using my chest for a pillow. I felt contented, relaxed. Idly, she began to caress my stomach and thighs. When she moved her hand to my groin, my cock slowly levitated like a cobra rising from a thicket. "You're blocking my view," said Misty. I pressed the off button on the remote and we went at it again.

In a couple of weeks we were practically living together, mostly at her place. She was a waitress saving up to go back to college. I had another sales job, which I hated. We both drank too much, but had plenty of sex and lots of laughs, and so for a while it was all good.

It went bad when I started to worry she might be fooling around on the side. Sometimes when I was on the road I would call her late at night and get the machine. "I took a pill," she'd later tell me. "I was out like a light."

At the restaurant there was a busboy she seemed too chummy with. And once when I returned from a trip earlier than expected, I went to her favorite watering hole and found her drunk and all over some guy at the bar. When she saw me standing behind her she seemed genuinely happy, and she dropped the guy like he was a turd. But seeing her that way had done its damage.

No matter what career she pretended to be pursuing, regardless of her stated plans to become an artist, or maybe a CEO, fucking was clearly her main interest. I would be at her place reading a book while she buzzed around the apartment, picking up dirty clothes, watering plants, checking the meatloaf, and all the while singing along with the blaring radio. I might come upon a passage that thrilled me, and I would turn off the radio and read it to her. "Isn't that wonderful?" I would say.

Misty would take the book from my hand and right away find the author's face on the jacket. By her expression I knew she was wondering what it might be like to fuck him. If the author was a woman, her gaze would turn contemptuous, hostile. "She looks like a whore," would be a typical comment.

I thought this through carefully, and decided I wasn't being an overly suspicious boyfriend. Often we'd watch TV and Tom Cruise or some cute guy with a guitar would come on, and Misty would say, "I hope you don't take offense at this, Fin, but I'd really like to jump his bones." Well, I thought, at least she's honest. "Not at all," I'd say. "Let me know when he's due to arrive. I'll make sure I'm on the road."

Misty divided people into four distinct groups: men she wanted to fuck (reciprocity assumed); men who wanted to fuck her, but in whom she had no interest (because they had repellent personalities or were grotesquely fat or otherwise physically disgusting); women who threatened her because they were attractive (most women, it seemed); and women who were not a threat because they lacked physical charms, or shared with her a deep, sisterly affection (very rare indeed). Children were not included, existing only as sudden apparitions to be hair-tousled and fawned over, or, theoretically, as roadblocks to her orgasms and other fun.

"No fucking way!" she said, the one time I half-seriously wondered if we might someday conceive a child. First there was the pain. "Try squirting a bowling ball through your dick," she said, "then multiply by a thousand." Next, the responsibility. "One mistake and you're tied down for what, eighteen fuckin' years? See ya!" And finally, the horror of being labeled a housewife and mother. Misty didn't want to waste her life changing diapers and going to Tupperware parties while hubby clinched deals at the office and strolled the fairways with his clients. She wanted to be a free-wheeling, tough-talking waitress who took art classes and could spend hours in a bar, if she felt like it, drinking construction workers and Navy Seals under the table before choosing the last one standing for a night of strenuous fucking.

Very shortly, then, the strong personality that I liked early on became abrasive and intolerable. But by the time I realized this, we had already progressed from frequent disagreements to constant arguing, and finally to a nasty physical fight during which I had the buttons ripped off my shirt and a tooth loosened by one of Misty's wind-milling punches, and Misty got herself badly bruised about the chest and shoulders when I pinned her hard to the floor.

I have tried to wipe these and other unpleasant details from my memory, and I have mostly succeeded but for one exception—the sound of an untended grilled cheese sandwich frying in a cast iron skillet. I'd been working on the grilled cheese when Misty came in drunk and looking pawed-over. I made an ugly comment and continued cooking my dinner. Misty said something in return, and when I ignored her she kicked me in the ass. Enraged, I hurled the spatula across the room and grabbed Misty by the arms, roughly propelling her out of the kitchen. She came flying back at me, her face contorted in fury, and we had the fight that would end our relationship for good. And through it all—as I had my face spat in, my eyes menaced by candy-apple red fingernails, my ears assailed by the banshee curses of the woman who had so easily fused her parts to mine in copulation, and Misty had her head banged against the linoleum floor, her wrists cruelly twisted, her character vilified by profane accusations of whorishness—the blackening grilled cheese sandwich sizzled in the skillet with an hysterical sibilance that sounded to me like the throaty cheers of spectators at a gladiatorial contest.

Recalling this and other memories of combative interactions with women, I was not eager to attend a bar, which, now that I was a non-drinker, I saw primarily as a place for ingratiating oneself with the opposite sex. But it seemed I had no choice; I was bedeviled by comrades who insisted I endure with them choking cigarette smoke and dim light and ear-blasting thumps of a jukebox, so I could be coerced into drinking gallons of beer that would make me stupid and sick, and all for team unity. How could I refuse?

We drove in Kenny Liebowitz's banged-up old Volvo to Sundowners, a cavernous bar with wooden picnic tables where patrons sat drinking pitchers of beer while devouring chicken wings and potato wedges and the like. I decided I would nurse a few beers during the course of the evening. I believed myself newly capable of temperance, and I would require liquid for the soothing of my tongue after its contact with the spicy-hot glaze on the wings, and the nerve-balm of alcohol to offset the twangy din of the country and western music played over and over on the jukebox.

I sat at the corner of a table with Ray and Ken and DeCurtis Johnson. Ken and DeCurtis scanned the room for available females, and I sipped my beer and listened to Ray elaborate on a theme he often brought up: the hard-heartedness of women.

I had met Ray's ex on a number of occasions. She was a pretty, petite blonde. She had skinny arms and an expressive mouth. A bundle of sex energy, I figured. She and Ray had a seven-year-old daughter who took lessons from a tall and dashing piano teacher, and Ray was certain the piano teacher was ready to step into his shoes. As beer made him sloshy, Ray spoke of the love he still felt for Barbara. He was of the mind that after her fling she would come to her senses. He loved her so much that he didn't care if she had another man's scent on her. But he was tormented by doubt.

"I don't know, Fin," he said. "It all seems so fucking hopeless. When I call her, she's like, 'Oh, it's you.' I'm not even in her head anymore. There's no pain in her voice."

"She's faking," I said. "She's in pain. She just doesn't want you to know it."

Liebowitz offered his two cents. "I don't know, man. Women are cold. They can put you out of their heads in a heartbeat."

"Hey," said DeCurtis, turning to face Ray, "don't listen to him. You never know how things'll work out."

"He's right," I said.

"Damn straight," said DeCurtis. "Shit, I knew this one couple fought all the time. Hated each other. One night things got so bad she packed her bags and screamed she was never coming back. So he opened the door for her and kicked her ass off the front porch, and she ended up face down on the flagstones. He felt sorry right away, you know? Tried to help her up. But she came up swearing and swinging at him. Ran off into the night cursing his very existence. The guy was miserable, man. In a fucking trance. So he gets out his shotgun and tries to blow his brains out. But he flinches at the last second and takes off his face."

"Jesus," said Liebowitz.

"Yeah, but listen. The bitch felt so bad she came back. Now she's his full time nurse. They never been closer, man."

"Thanks," said Ray. "You guys are making me feel a lot better."

DeCurtis Johnson had a lot of stories. A highly touted athlete out of the Chicago projects, he'd gotten a free ride at Ohio State as a defensive back. Drafted by the Bears, he'd been cut in training camp for a lack of intensity. The thing is, DeCurtis wasn't sure he wanted to be a football player. Ever since he'd learned what college professors did for a living he knew it was the best scam going. These guys had a life of leisure. They taught a few classes, went to conferences, took sabbaticals. That was for him. And he had the brains to pull it off. A born mimic and raconteur, he was comfortable talking trash or Tolstoy. He actually liked reading and studying and thought the life of the mind more stimulating than trying to knock people out on the football field. In his senior year he had fallen in love with semiotics, and was now working on his master's degree in the hope of teaching it. One day while dressing in the locker room he told this to fellow defensive back Carthage

Lee. Lee said, "Semi-*what?* Hell, nigger, teach the *whole* subject."

And DeCurtis had an interesting hobby: white folks. He found the manners and trappings of the Caucasian lifestyle fascinating. He studied old Ozzie and Harriet tapes, and sometimes, just for fun, would spend a week or so talking like Ozzie or Rick or David Nelson. It was easy. All he had to do was begin every sentence with "Oh."

"Oh, hi Lou, hi Fin."

Hey DeCurtis, where'd you put that *Hustler* I loaned you?

"Oh, it's right here in my locker."

And so on. He collected old record albums by Perry Como and Steve Lawrence. And when he was in one of those Nelson Family moods, he went around in saddle shoes, tan chinos, and a button down Oxford shirt under a robin's-egg blue cardigan. The first time Sal Gargano saw him dressed like this, he said, "Holy shit, Johnson, you look like Pat Boone in blackface."

DeCurtis loved cardigans, which he collected at rummage sales and thrift shops. It was his plan that the first time he took an interception back for a touchdown, a co-

conspirator would run out on the field to give him a cardigan which he would put on over his uniform. No jive-ass dances or hidden sharpies, but an homage to his field of study.

Since it was Friday night, Sundowners was packed, and especially with Cossacks. We had plenty of steam to let off and things became loud and boisterous. Kicker Reg Hastings, a tough SOB from Manchester, England, was teaching the Cossacks some of the ridiculous chants he and his mates would bellow in the pubs back home. It was good fun, but I could see that some of the locals weren't digging it. A few shit-kicker types at the bar were sizing us up, trying to look mean in their muscle shirts and cowboy boots and hillbilly pompadours and side-burns. But they hardly registered with us; we were too many and too big. There would be no rumble that night. Not even after a frothily drunk Hastings yelled, *"Dead ants!"*

Now this was something I had known about—and sometimes got dragged into—since my freshman year in college. It was new to Hastings, though, and he loved it and tried to get the Cossacks to do it whenever possible. The deal was this: You were out partying with your buddies—at a bar, a dance, wherever—and if one of the gang suddenly hollered "Dead ants!" you and the others were duty bound to fall immediately to the floor and assume the inert, crumpled posture of a dead ant. You had to do it. It was part of the unwritten code. You would lie there for as long as it took—until the guy who'd called it gave the all clear—while people were stepping over you and being generally inconvenienced. This was best done at a wedding or other formal engagement, as the idea was to annoy the squares. My guess is the genius who first came up with this plan had been inspired by the sight of the carnage on an ant battlefield. It was the sort of goof greatly enjoyed by males in their twenties. But I was no longer in my twenties, and I wished that Hastings had not sounded the call. I was a player, though, and had no choice. I couldn't let my teammates down. So I curled up on the dirty stinking floor in my nice L. L. Bean polo shirt and prayed nobody would step on my face. I was glad, at least, that I'd had a few beers. I was buzzed and a little tired. I would make it through "Dead Ants."

On the drive back to the dorm, Liebowitz took a detour up a dirt road that brought us to the top of a hill overlooking Centerport. Some of the guys wanted to polish off a six-pack they'd bought before leaving Sundowners. We sat there a while, drinking and winding down the night. I got out and walked a few paces from the car and unleashed a long, satisfying piss into the weeds while all around me katydids exulted in the warm dark. Behind me I heard muffled voices from the car. A soft wind rustled the weeds, and in the distance I could see the lights of the city flickering under the black sky. Loneliness came to me, then, like a stab in the heart. I knew there was no way to stop this from happening every so often. No cure for it, either.

I shook away the last drops of pee, zipped up, and walked wearily back to the car.

I slept deeply and awoke at dawn. On Sunday there was no practice until the afternoon, so I lay in bed for a few minutes thinking what I would do with the free hours ahead of me.

I had no hangover. I got up and stretched, fully nude (I always sleep in the nude). In a tree beyond the window a cardinal sat singing its heart out.

Being a gentleman, I put on a bathrobe before padding down the hall to the can. No one else seemed to be awake. I stepped into the shower and turned the hot water way up. The place had good water pressure, and I luxuriated under the stinging hot needles of spray. I thought of singing in the shower, but nothing came to me. That was fine; it pleased me just to hear the sizzle and splash of the water. I was starting to feel pretty good.

I didn't even mind very much when offensive tackle Paul Facemeyer came in and commenced a tragic bowel movement in one of the stalls. While drying off, I had to listen to the poor sap groaning and expelling thunderclaps of gas during his struggle with the wages of nocturnal gluttony. This was precisely the sort of incident that could have soured my mood, but on this morning I felt so chipper that it didn't bother me at all. Still, I hustled right out of there.

I got to the dining hall by nine, and took a seat with Lou Levine and Sal Gargano. They'd already finished their Danish and dried-out scrambled eggs and were arguing about sex.

Both men had wives they'd left at home because their kids were still in school, and neither was inclined to fool around, so they were quite naturally discussing masturbation.

"You're wrong, Lou," said Sal. "Every time you jack off you squander vital energy you could be saving up for conjugal weekends. Me, I keep my hands away from my dick at all times. When the wife gets here I'm like a teenager. She walks bow-legged for days."

Lou glanced idly in my direction, watched me shoveling forkfuls of ham scrapple into my mouth. I had a good appetite that morning. "Let's get the opinion of a younger man," said Lou. "Tell us, Fin, when's the last time you flogged the bishop, and how did you feel about it?"

Sal interjected. "More to the point, when's the last time he got laid. Then we can ask him about his jack-off habits."

I swallowed a mouthful of scrapple, took a long hit of orange juice. "You know, I was in a swell mood when I sat down here."

"Okay," said Lou, "forget about your personal life. Just give us your opinion. If you had a wife and you couldn't be with her for a while, would you masturbate regularly, or store it up for the conjugal visits?

Someone had left a Sunday paper on the bench next to me. I extracted the comics. "I don't think it's necessary to store it up," I said.

"Of course not," said Lou. "Long as you get enough sleep and fresh air, your body makes all the semen you could ever want. And by masturbating, you bring peace into your life."

I concentrated on the comics. I'd grown up with *Peanuts,* and in later years enjoyed *Bloom County* and *Calvin and Hobbes* and *The Far Side.* But now all I ever read is *Family Circus.* I find it comforting to see ghostly grandparents in the clouds, looking down over the little munchkins.

Lou continued. "In one of his letters, William Burroughs said, 'I write to you with the philosophic serenity of an empty scrotum.' He nailed it."

"Who's William Burroughs?" asked Sal.

I said, "He was a junkie. And a fag."

"Yes," said Lou, "and his scrotum had been emptied by an Arab lad, if I remember correctly. But so what? A woman would have given him the same result. Peace."

"I don't know," said Sal. "When you start quoting junkie fags, you lose credibility."

I pushed the paper aside and stood up with my tray. "Just once," I said, "I'd like to have a meal where I don't have to listen to people talk about masturbating, or shitting."

Sal looked genuinely confused. "Who said anything about shitting?"

I carried my tray to the drop-off table and left the building. The day was bright and beautiful, but my mood sagged a little. It hadn't been the table talk about jerking-off. Hell, I was used to that sort of thing. It was that goddamn *Family Circus*. The one-panel drawing showed the family getting out of their station wagon after a drive back from vacation. They were all smudged and disheveled, carrying luggage and sleeping bags. Rolled-up newspapers were on the lawn, which needed cutting. Their house, framed by a purple sunset, was an ordinary split-level job. But they shared a thought bubble, and in this bubble their home was drawn as a golden palace.

I wanted that kind of life. A loving wife, kids, a home where it all came together. With Annette there had been a chance. I wondered if it would be the only chance I'd ever get.

During my rambles through Centerport I had eyeballed many attractive women. I saw them at the mall, the supermarket, convenience stores. Jogging on bicycle paths. Power-walking on suburban streets. Talking, arms folded, with Jiffy-Lube mechanics. Dumping newspapers and plastic jugs at the recycling center. They were everywhere. But they all seemed to be taken. They wore diamond-studded wedding rings, were loading grocery bags into a minivan full of yammering tots, or they appeared in public squired by the bland, fortunate husband. The fingers of the joggers and power-walkers could not easily be scoped for rings; their don't-fuck-with-me concentration made them unapproachable. There were three women who worked in the offices of the Cossacks. Two were plump and dowdy, and the third, a looker, had already started dating Reg Hastings because she liked his British accent. A pair of football groupies had stationed themselves at Sundowners and were working their way through the roster, but they were not for me. I was looking for a relationship with a probability of permanence, and I don't much care for women with big hair and frosty makeup at any rate.

Women on the go, staccatoing out of a shoe store at the mall, for example, I could not bring myself to accost. That took nerve, which I seemed to have lost. Fondly, I remembered earlier days when I would think nothing of hustling alongside such a woman, politely inquiring about her choice of footwear, offering to carry her parcels, trying to get her phone number.

It occurred to me that I might use a little spiral notebook to keep a record of the pretty women I saw. At the drug store one day I actually had such a notebook in my hand, but when I visualized myself frantically scribbling in it after, say, a pleasant exchange with a waitress, I knew that such a course of action would be too creepy for words. So I filed auspicious sightings away in my memory, and one above all the others kept nagging at me.

An avid reader, I am no stranger to the local library. During my first week in Centerport I had acquired a library card. To the best of my knowledge I was the only Cossack who had one. Even Kenny Liebowitz, who read books and fancied himself an intellectual, appeared confused when I asked him if he'd ever been to the Centerport library.

"Library? Why the hell would I go to the library?" He had two boxes of books in the trunk of his car, and when he felt like reading he would root around for a suitable volume, most likely something left over from a college course in American Literature or Man and the Environment. If he wanted something new, he'd buy a mass-market paperback thriller at the supermarket.

Once I made the mistake of asking Ray Whipple the same question. Ray fixed me with a look of pure incomprehension, as if I had suddenly begun speaking in tongues. "Never mind," I said. "It was a sick joke."

Anyway, as far as I was concerned the whole team and every other horny, eligible male in town could stay away from the library forever, since there was a librarian there that I wanted for myself.

She was a tall, slender blonde with high cheekbones. She had blue eyes, long lashes and a snub nose. The first time I saw her she was talking with a little boy who was doing his homework at a table next to her desk. I browsed the new book section and kept my ears peeled; I figured out soon enough that the boy was her son. They were joking with each other, and suddenly the woman erupted in laughter, a beautiful sound. That was a treat. So often I have heard a pretty girl open her mouth and let loose with a laugh that sounds like Mr. Ed on helium. It was a small library, and wherever I wandered I could hear the woman talking to her son. The tenor of their bantering suggested Mom and Son going it alone, with a divorced or deceased dad out of the picture, although this was all conjecture on my part. I selected a mystery set in Boston and took it to the check-out desk.

Upon closer inspection, the woman was even more attractive than I had first thought. Her hair was short but not too short—not dykey. She wore a peach-colored cotton T-shirt with a scalloped neckline, and an emerald pendant. She greeted me with a bright hello, took my card in her long delicate fingers, and checked out the book. When she gave me back the book and my card, I noticed that her nails were perfectly manicured and lightly painted a color that matched her T-shirt. The woman had class.

She chirped the due date at me, and for a moment our eyes locked. I wanted the moment to last, but she looked away effortlessly and spoke to the elderly woman fidgeting with her books behind me.

That was the first time I'd seen her. On two subsequent occasions she had been at the desk to check out my books, but I hadn't said anything more than a thank-you. Now, as I idled away the rest of Sunday morning in my room, I swore that my next trip to the library would be different. I would wait for the right moment, and I would be witty and charming. And then I would ask her out.

But I ran into a snafu. On Monday after practice I showered, dressed nice, and hurried to the library only to find that the girl wasn't there. A middle-aged woman with thin lips and cold gray eyes manned the desk. I was stuck. What could I do, go up to her and ask, "Pardon me, but when will the pretty blonde be back?"

A return trip on Tuesday was out. There was an evening meeting in preparation for the home opener on Wednesday night. I had to forget about the library for a few days.

The founders of the NFA had known what they were doing when they scheduled all the games for Wednesday nights. It was the one day of the week when there was no football being played anywhere. Well, there was also Tuesday, but that was right on the heels of Monday Night Football. Games every Wednesday night would give football junkies a middle-of-the-week fix.

I was impressed by the hoopla for the opening game against the Wheeling Dervishes. Mr. Mankopf had put together a marching band and a cheerleading squad, and when we took the field for the first time, we tore one-by-one through an enormous paper Cossack logo while over the loudspeaker our names, positions, and colleges were announced by Michael Buffer, the "Let's get ready to rumble!" guy. He must have cost Mr. Mankopf a pretty penny.

I saw an ESPN truck beyond the sidelines and wondered if I'd get to meet The Boomer, a famous, very likeable announcer with a big beefy head. But then I remembered that The

Boomer was strictly a studio man. More likely there would be in attendance one of those hot female broadcasters who had long ago infiltrated ESPN and the other networks. As far as that goes, I had never played the game at the level where you could expect all kinds of strangers—including women—in the locker room. I was used to shedding my clothes at my locker and not worrying about the few seconds that my pecker was exposed before it disappeared behind a towel. Would I now have to be more careful? To be perfectly honest, I am not large in the schlong department, and I didn't need some chick smirking at me while I stood next to, say, our quarterback Drew Danielson, a freak whose penis dangles practically at knee level. Not that I'm a pecker checker, but there are some things you just can't help noticing. In a football locker room, for instance, there are always a few guys whose big dicks sway like truncheons when they stroll imperiously to the shower, towels draped over their shoulders. It is my observation that it doesn't matter how successful you are in sports, business, or with the ladies—if you have a small dick, you walk to the shower with your towel wrapped around your waist. Of course there are exceptions like Ray Whipple, happy souls with dicks so tiny they look like acorns (especially after shower shrinkage), but who stand there laughing and joking with the rest of the guys while toweling off their chests and shoulders, not giving a crap that their little dicks bob up and down like a rabbit's nose.

While we're on the subject, it has been my experience that most women don't seem to care about size. On the other hand, I know there are some—a minority, I have always hoped—who really, *really* want to be filled up with a huge cock, and nothing else will do. I expressed this very thought once to a girl I wasn't sure I'd given a good enough time. She was lying next to me in bed, smoking a ciga-rette. "Sorry, Fin," she said, "we're the major-ity." Majority or not, they make enough noise to keep guys with small or medium-sized dicks off balance.

But these were passing thoughts. I was settling myself into the electric moment that precedes the game. In the locker room Lou had delivered a short speech, reminding eve-ryone of the primary objective: to execute. If we blocked and tackled and ran and covered the way we'd been taught in practice, we would win. He said, "This is the first step in a journey that will last not only for the season, but for the rest of your lives. So make it a big one."

When the cheers died down, Paul Facemeyer jerked his thumb at Bobby Hertzig and said, "Hey, Coach, Bobby wants to know if he heard you right. Did you say 'Take the big one?'"

I love the opening kickoff. For my money, it's the most exciting moment in all of sports. And if it's on a chilly night with everyone hopping up and down to stay warm, so much the better.

I watched the Wheeling kicker run to the tee, and heard the drawing in of one huge collective breath, and then the expulsion of it with a roar as the ball sailed end-over-end up into the black sky of night.

Walt Watson took the ball at the three-yard line and veered to the right, where he found a seam and turned up field and burst into an open space. Watson was our fastest guy, and the Wheeling special teamers looked clumsy and slow as they lunged at him. The last Dervish with a shot was a linebacker who was taking the correct angle to cut Watson off at the fifty. But this linebacker, a rookie from a division three college somewhere out in the desolate Northern Plains, had never seen the likes of Walt Watson, a Florida whippet who claimed to be a foundling from a higher dimension where everything happened twice as fast. Watson turned on the burners and would have run past the linebacker without a flourish, but an animal cruelty concomitant with blazing speed compelled him to an almost imperceptible inside feint—just enough to transform the linebacker from a reasonably graceful athlete into a stumblebum with the stiff, awkward gait of a reanimated corpse. And then Walt Watson was gone, and suddenly we were up 6-0.

In the end zone special teams players Del Bennett and Sean Madigan jumped on Watson's back and knocked him to the ground. In football you show your appreciation for a teammate by practically breaking his neck.

Wheeling had trouble scoring because their quarterback, Darrell Raney, was forty-years-old, downright elderly by football standards. He would stand in the pocket like a man watching a sunset, easy pray for our blitzing linebackers and sack-happy defensive ends. On two successive plays Raney was smushed by C-faw McClintock for losses totaling 34 yards.

When C-faw ran his hyperventilating self to the sidelines everyone crowded around to high-five him and pound him on the back. I was glad to see it, too, because C-faw McClintock is one of the nicest guys you'd ever want to meet, a gentle old-country white boy from the backwoods of Tennessee who'd taken a ribbing all his life on account of having a head with an odd shape to it. C-faw's head is wide on top, squashed in the middle, and lantern-jawed at the bottom. A college teammate had said he looked like a creature from another world. The nickname stuck and was shortened to its anagram, C-faw. His real name is Jeremiah, but I never heard anyone call him that.

At the start of the second half we were up 17-0, and it looked like we would dominate. But in football there is a mysterious force called momentum, which can change like the affections of a teenage girl, and eventually it kicked in on the Wheeling side. Raney got his mind focused and started hitting his favorite receiver, Jarvis Eldred, all of 5' 7" and 164 pounds, who danced and threaded his way through our scattered defenders for huge gains. Eldred scored from the twelve, and then midway through the fourth quarter their safety, Epcot Fitzgerald, picked off an errant pass by Danielson and took it all the way in for a touchdown, grinning wide and holding the ball high over his head to taunt guard Paul Facemeyer, who at first had given pursuit, but now stood helplessly with his arms at his side, watching like a eunuch at a gang-bang.

It came down to the last play of the game. Two seconds left, Cossacks leading 17-14; Wheeling with the ball on their own thirty-eight, too far away to kick a game-tying field goal. Only one option remained. It would be a play that is every defensive coach's nightmare: the dreaded Hail-Mary. Sure, the Hail-Mary is low percentage. You throw the ball high in the air, say your prayers to the Blessed Virgin, and hope that when it comes down in the end zone one of your guys will grab it. Most of the time this doesn't work. But the horror is in the awful suddenness of it. Losing a game in such a way can break a team's spirit. And it isn't only the leaping wideouts you have to worry about, but the officials. Six players colliding under the ball in the end-zone—an entanglement of jostling limbs and flying elbows—can lead to a pass-interference call. And since the game cannot end on a penalty, the offense will get the ball on the one-yard line, with the chance to punch it in even with no time showing on the clock.

So when Raney lofted that final pass and Preston Qualters, Wheeling's 6-foot-6 receiver, positioned himself in the end zone, the Cossacks were howling and grimacing on the sideline, willing the ball into the next county with tortured body English.

The ball didn't make it into the next county, but it did travel a fair distance out of the end zone after bouncing with a loud *thunk* off Qualters' helmet.

And just like that, we had won our home opener.

After the game Teddy Mankopf entered the happy locker room. I must say that Mr. Mankopf was unlike certain famous owners who feel the need to push their weight around—their *financial* weight—in an arena where they would be bottom dogs if matters were settled with hand-to-hand combat. He seemed comfortable with himself, and whenever he came to practice he stood off to the side and did not get in anyone's face, though he always made pleasant conversation if you said hello to him.

His family had been in the funeral business for two generations, and when Mr. Mankopf senior passed away, Teddy decided to make some changes. Not everyone, he reasoned, wanted to go through the rigmarole of the burial process. People generally went along with it because there was pressure to conform in the hour of grief. So Teddy Mankopf took a daring step. Throughout the Northeast, he set up a string of quick-stop mortuaries. No fuss, no frills. The deceased were cremated without pomp, and a tasteful notice was sent to friends and relatives. The ashes were dumped into cardboard boxes and could be stored in perpetuity at one of the mortuarial warehouses. Naturally he had many critics. Church people hated him, and so did other morticians until they realized that *Peaceful Passings,* which is what he called the franchise, was an idea worth buying into. One especially bitter critic, a devout Catholic and newspaper columnist in Scranton, said why not sell coffee and donuts, too, and call it *Gulp n' Grieve.* But like all visionaries, Teddy Mankopf was immune to naysaying, and now, some years later, had become more successful than ever.

You wouldn't have sized him up for a guy who heard the *ca-ching* of the cash register every time somebody croaked. He was big and healthy looking. The tan on his face and his bleached white hair suggested plenty of time near the water, or on the golf course. At sixty-three he could have passed for fifty. He was divorced and had a beautiful young mistress, but he didn't flaunt her. We had only seen her once, hanging on his arm while they watched practice from the sidelines.

After showering and dressing I went with Lou and punter Austin Goudy to a place called *Joey's,* where we drank cokes and ate slices of pizza.

"Did you see that jacket?" asked Lou, referring to the dark green sport coat Mr. Mankopf had worn. "Pure cashmere. The man knows how to dress. I hear he has his shirts custom-made by some fancy haberdasher in New York."

"Amazing," said Goudy. "And to think a guy like that was standing there talking to C-faw McClintock." He bit off a shred of pizza and chewed thoughtfully, shaking his head at the wonder of such a mismatched confabulation.

"What about his shoes?" I asked.

Coach Levine sipped a large measure of coke through a straw and stared at me. "What *about* the shoes?"

"Are *they* custom-made, too?" I was curious. If I ever strike it rich, one of the first things I'll do is have a pair of shoes—hell, two or three pairs—custom made. I've had pretty good luck with the store-bought variety, but every now and then I'll get a pair that doesn't fit right even after being broken in. It seems to me that one of the great luxuries in life would be to walk around never once thinking about how your feet are feeling.

But there was something wrong with Lou. His normally pleasant smile twisted into a sneer. He pushed away his paper plate and his big plastic cup, like it was some kind of little ceremony he had to do before getting up to knock my teeth out. "It's always shoes with you, isn't it? It always comes back to the shoes."

Goudy pouched his mouthful of pizza into one cheek. "I know what you mean, Lou," he said innocently. "I remember this job counselor telling me that your shoes are the first thing a boss sees when you come into the room, and the last thing he looks at when you leave."

Lou ignored him. "Is it some kind of fetish?" he asked.

I understood. This was a man in his forties, mature and responsible, the head coach and general manager of a professional football team, and in everyone's estimation an extremely together guy. But he had pressures, and he needed to vent now and then, and apparently something about shoes could set him off. I remembered the time in the motel room with the ugly shoes. The whole thing was very fucked up.

"Lou," I said, "like I told you before, I don't give a damn about your shoes or any other item of clothing you care to display, no matter how hideous."

"It's not *my* shoes we're discussing."

I wiped the grease from my fingers with one of those flimsy napkins they provide at pizza joints. "Okay," I said, "you win. I won't hide it anymore. Back in my room I've got a suitcase full of men's shoes. Wing-tips, bedroom slippers, dirty smelly old sneakers. I've been stealing them from locker rooms for years. You want to know exactly what I do with 'em?"

"Come on!" said Goudy. "I'm tryin' to eat here."

Lou allowed the matter to drop. He was not, after all, an actual psychopath.

I suddenly felt tired, out of energy. I sensed this in my companions as well. The three of us sat on vinyl seats under harsh lights and finished the rest of the pizza. We chewed and drank in silence, lost in thought. In a booth across the aisle a young couple gazed into each other's eyes over the leavings of a rigatoni dinner. They were an average-looking couple, the guy a slightly overweight, the girl with a nose a little too big. But they were in love. You could see it in the way they looked at each other. When they got up to leave, the man put his hand lightly on the girl's back while she fiddled with her purse and buttoned her coat. It was the simplest, most casual of gestures, but the sight of it gave me a warm feeling in my heart. And then almost right away it made me feel empty. Seeing people in love will do that to you when there's nobody in your life.

The librarian was in my head when I woke up the next morning. I lay in my solitary bed thinking of her, and an old memory came to me.

It's April in Boston, and I'm walking to Fenway Park to catch a Red Sox-Yankees game. I'm oblivious to my surroundings until a sweet voice chimes in my ear. A young woman is suddenly at my side, asking for directions to Kenmore Square. I turn to face her, and find myself dumbstruck by her beauty. She has the look of a country girl, a farmer's daughter, perhaps. There is a wind-swept, sun-kissed quality about her. Her strawberry-blonde hair is tied in pigtails, her smile is artless, her skin unblemished. She wears a white sundress mottled with blue cornflowers, and her innocent feet rest snugly in white matching sandals. Pointing in the direction she must go, I tell her she is only a couple of blocks from Kenmore Square. At such happy news her smile brightens, and in the April sunlight her vivid blue eyes sparkle with a simple joy, and I am overcome with a desire to hold her in my arms.

And what action do I take? None. Slowly (*reluctantly*, I would later recall, in misery), the girl disengages herself from our meeting. She walks away with a single, smiling, backward glance that every corpuscle in my pounding heart receives as an invitation to spend eternity with her. But I do nothing.

Remembering this now, writhing with anguish in the chaos of my bedclothes, I swear that I will not make the same mistake again.

I walked into the library with the mystery, the one set in Boston, as so many of them are. Gently I placed it on the desk, giving it a little shove in the direction of the librarian. She picked it up and looked at the dust jacket. "Any good?" she asked.

I gave her my best smile. "Not good enough for me to read all the way to the end."

The librarian smiled back and nodded. "I know what you mean. It's tough these days to find something worth reading."

"Chilling words from someone who works all day surrounded by books."

She graced me with the lovely laugh I had heard before. Things were proceeding nicely. Much better than I'd expected. Like Goober from *The Andy Griffith Show*, who in one episode approached his date's doorstep armed with a crib sheet of conversational gambits, I was prepared with a number of ice-breakers. But the girl had spoken first, and now it was smooth sailing. I extended my hand to her. "By the way, I come in here often enough, so I might as well introduce myself. I'm Fin Connors."

"Pleased to meet you, Fin," she said, taking my hand and giving it a gentle but firm shake. "But I knew your name from your card."

"Of course."

"And I'm Laura Barnett." She passed the book under the scanner, checking it in. "You have an unusual name," she said.

"It's short for Finbar. I'm Irish on both sides."

"Poor you," said Laura. "I'm kidding," she quickly added. "My mother's name was

Gogarty. Mary Margaret. So I know a little about being Irish."

There was a lull, and I knew it could be fatal. One more second and she'd be doing something else, and my chance would be gone.

"I couldn't help noticing you with a little boy the last time I was here," I said. "Your son, I presume?"

"Yes," said Laura. "That's Cody. Best thing in my life."

"Great," I said. "I mean, kids are really great. I don't have any myself, of course. But I used to work with kids." Now it was going badly. I was meandering. "Anyway, listen, I play for the Cossacks. You've heard of them, right?"

"Sure I have."

"Well, I've got some free tickets. We get them before every game and I don't know anyone here in town, so if your boy, if Cody likes football, maybe he'd like to go. I mean with you, of course. I have a ticket for you, too, if you want it." Suave. Real suave.

But it was okay. I could tell by her face that she was pleased with the offer. "Are you sure?" she said. "Cody does like football. He's not the greatest athlete in the world, but I know he'd love to go."

I dug into my pocket for the tickets. "My pleasure. They're for the next home game, two weeks from Wednesday. The Manchester Purple Demons, a very good team, we're told."

Laura accepted the tickets and we talked for a few more minutes. She wanted to know what position I played. I told her, and her comments and questions indicated that she knew something about the game. I would have continued talking about myself, which I like to do, but was interrupted by a woman with an armload of paperback romances to be checked out. So I stood aside and waited. When Laura had scanned the last of the books, a bodice-ripper entitled *The Callous Dragoon,* I stepped back up to the desk and made my move.

"Maybe we could do dinner sometime. I mean if the idea appeals to you."

As the words were leaving my mouth, I realized I had failed to inquire first about her marital status. But so what? If she said she was married or seeing someone, no big deal. Back in the old days it happened all the time.

But she was not married or seeing someone. "Sure," she said. "I haven't been on a date in a long time. Let me give you my number." She took a scrap of paper and wrote on it with a pencil.

God, did I like this girl. Pretty, bright, and no head games. "I'll call you after the Manchester game," I said. "We'll go someplace nice."

On Wednesday we traveled to Vermont and easily defeated the Rutland Moose, 40-6. I thought Moose a ridiculous name for a team, and so did the other Cossacks. From the sidelines they kept yelling, "Where's Bullwinkle?" Judson Trask was the star of the night, scoring on runs of 23, 45, and 60 yards. I got in the game with just a few minutes left and caught a 12-yard pass from backup quarterback Mike Ponsonby.

Everything was fine except for one minor incident. Kilmer Joyce tackled the Moose quarterback for a big loss, but in so doing twisted his ankle. It turned out to be nothing serious, but it caused him a lot of immediate pain, and as he hobbled to the sidelines he cried out, *"Jesus fuckin' Christ!"*

96

When Hollis Daft heard this he became agitated. It was the one thing he could not tolerate—yoking the name of his Lord and Savior to the f-word. Hollis was a veteran player and coach, so he didn't exactly have virgin ears. But he was a born-again Southern Baptist, and if you brought Jesus into your foul-mouthed expostulations, he would get after you about it. He tried that with Kilmer, but Kilmer was in too much pain at the moment to give a damn. Hollis complained to Lou, and Lou just looked at him like he was nuts. So Hollis sulked for the rest of the night and even into the next day.

Kilmer and I talked about this during the ride back to Centerport. Kilmer Joyce was a three-hundred-pound giant of a man from rural Louisiana, a dignified African American who in earlier times would have been called "a credit to his race." He was without malice or prejudice, treating everyone he met with respect and kindness, except on the field of play, where he was a one-man search-and-destroy mission. He was feeling a little bad about upsetting Hollis Daft. "The man shouldn't get so bent outa shape over a little cussin'," he said. "Shoot, my daddy used to say Jesus fuckin' Christ so much I thought *fuckin'* was the Lord's middle name. Got me in trouble at school, too. Nun asked me who's the son of God, and I say Jesus fuckin' Christ. When I found out what fuckin' actually meant, I *still* thought it was his middle name. Way I saw it, if your rap was so slick people thought you was the son of God, you'd be fuckin' so much it'd be *your* middle name *too.*"

I advised Kilmer to keep that little story to himself, especially around Coach Daft.

Hollis Daft was a pretty good offensive co-ordinator, but it was common knowledge that in his youth he'd been a royal pain in the ass, before an incident tainted his purity and made him shut up about the Lord once in a while. It happened when Hollis was quarter-backing Memphis in the old USFL. He was having a decent year, but he was also pissing everyone off with his holier-than-thou lectures on Jesus and the Bible. He was such a godly man that he wouldn't even take a crap without saying a prayer first. But what really got his teammates in a lather was his determination to put an end to all the indiscriminate fornicating they enjoyed. He threatened to expose them all, especially the married guys who liked a little poon on the side. When the head coach got wind of this, he had a sit-down with Hollis and that was the end of that. Regardless, some of the players got together and decided that Hollis Daft was a time bomb who could go off in the vicinity of their dicks at any moment. He had to be taught a lesson.

There was a linebacker on the team, Vic "Frenchy" DeVito, whose hobby was oral sex. DeVito had an incredible collection of oral porno that he toted around in a duffel bag, and even though he was Italian they called him Frenchy because, as everyone knows, the French invented the blow job. Anyway, one night Frenchy and a few of his pals kid-napped Hollis Daft and took him to a motel out in the boonies. They put duct tape over his mouth and tied him to the bed. Then a blonde, leggy hooker came into the room and went to work on him. Since Frenchy was running the show (he even had a video cam-era fired up), most of what the hooker did was in the oral department. According to the story, Hollis tried to resist, rolling his eyes and mumbling what sounded like prayers under the duct tape. But the hooker had too much skill. And she took direction well. At the last moment she lifted her face from Hollis's groin and watched with an evil smile as Frenchy the auteur zoomed in for what in the parlance of the pornographer is called the "cum shot." Then came the *real* climax of the film. The hooker reached up and pulled off her wig, revealing a brush cut, and dropped her miniskirt, showing that *she* was unmistakably a *he*.

Perhaps the story was untrue. I do know that Frenchy DeVito blew out his knee in practice shortly after the alleged incident. Frenchy and his porn-filled duffel bag drifted out of football. Legend has it he became a down-and-out drunk in his hometown of Cleveland, which makes you wonder if some kind of payback from the Lord was going down.

One thing making me happy was the fact that I was doing a very good job as a Cossack. I had a hell of an attitude, had thrown myself heart and soul into the work. This has not always been the case, as should be obvious from what I've mentioned so far about my work history. It took me a long time to mature, to understand that work in itself, no matter how menial, is good for the soul.

My brother Kevin used to have a poster on his wall that was a series of cartoon panels showing this weird hippie guru named Mr. Natural doing the dishes, of all things. It starts off with Mr. Natural frowning and muttering over the pile of filthy dishes in the sink. You can see the grease and bits of leftover food and a couple of flies buzzing around. So he rolls up his sleeves and gets to work, and a few panels later when he's made a dent he's actually whistling to himself. The clean dishes end up in the dish drainer, dripping and spotless, and Mr. Natural, a homely dude about five feet tall, walks away with a big smile on his face and says, "Another job well done."

The first time I saw it I told Kevin I thought it was a stupid poster. He gave me this tolerant smile and said it was about the Zen of work. I told him I'd read a book or two in my life, and I knew what Zen was but I still thought the poster was stupid. "He's smiling now," I said, "but after another blow-out weekend he'll have more dirty dishes to do. It never ends."

I actually came to enjoy Mr. Natural. (Kevin had some of the comic books lying around, and they weren't half bad once you got into them.) But I was usually too pissed off and bored to go into a Zen trance while doing most of my lousy jobs. Coaching at the athletic camp was good. That I liked. But all the other jobs I could have done without. I won't bore you with a list of what they were, except to tell you that one time I won a contest when a bunch of us were sitting around talking about how quickly we'd been fired from or had quit various jobs. Nobody can beat me, I said. I had the shortest job in all history. There was scoffing all around until I told the story.

It was my first summer home from college, and I was looking forward to drinking with friends and sleeping late. I thought I could live at home and eat for free, but mom had other ideas. She grew tired of seeing her powerfully built son standing in his underwear in the kitchen, scratching his ass and checking the fridge for leftovers he might enjoy while planning another day of leisure. It was put to me that I must earn my keep. This was before I had hooked up with Lou at his camp, so I had no recourse but to check the want ads. The biggest ad was for McDonald's.

So I got into my wobbly azure Plymouth and drove to the nearest Golden Arches. I walked through the door at eleven a.m., just as things were starting to get busy. The previous night I had been drunk, as usual, so I had a headache and a parched mouth. There were three lines of impatient customers and the harried clerks were barking orders to the fry cooks in the rear. Like a hesitant groom I wandered behind the counter, where I was immediately confronted by a tall man wearing a bow tie and a little cap on his head.

"I saw your ad for help wanted," I said.

He took two seconds to look me up and down. "Terrific. What are you doing right now?"

Stunned, I answered truthfully. "Nothing."

"You're hired." He pointed to a room in the back. "You'll find an apron and a hat in there. We can do the paperwork later. Let's go."

He hurried away and I walked miserably into the room, where I indeed found a little

McDonald's hat and an apron. Both were clean and crisp from the laundry. I pried open the hat and placed it on my head. I picked up the apron and felt like crying. This was all happening too fast. I had expected an interview, a written psychological test, a handshake and the assurance that I was an excellent candidate, and then a few days to relax before receiving the congratulatory phone call. Suddenly I realized that this storage room had a door that opened onto the back parking lot, a door that had been left open, presumably for ventilation. Silently declaring myself unhired, I removed the cap and walked briskly out the back door. My only regret was that I didn't get to see the look on the manager's face when he realized I was gone.

Well, that's the kind of dumb kid I was back then, and for a few years more, I'm afraid. But not these days. Older and wiser, I understand that the world doesn't owe me a living and that nobody is going to take care of me. Which is why I was well pleased when Lou asked me to go with him on a weekend trip to scout Duane Dunkle. I had told Lou I might want to be a scout one day, and now he was going to let me get my feet wet.

This Duane Dunkle was a high school kid in a little town in the Finger Lakes region, about a two-hour drive from Centerport. He was a senior and had declared that he wanted to bypass the college experience and go right into pro football. The national media was interested for a couple of reasons.

First, the kid was 6'8", 370, an offensive tackle who pancaked everyone in his path. He played defense, too, and went after ball carriers with such ferocity that the high school sports editor, in a youthful frenzy of wordplay, had once described him as "Mighty Joe Young tearing natives limb from limb." Since Dunkle wasn't black, there had been no PC uproar about comparing him to a giant gorilla. Second, this sort of collegiate bypass was unheard of in the world of football. Baseball players went from high school to the minor leagues all the time, and in recent years a whole lot of teenaged hoop stars had been snapped up by NBA teams, much to the chagrin of college coaches, fans, and sportswriters who regarded the Final Four as a sacred rite. But the grand poobahs of the NFL would have none of this heresy. Unthinkable that a young man should come into the league without benefit of a college education. Of course the fact that some of these young men were thugs, others would never get a diploma, and a handful would prove to be functionally illiterate never counted for much. A whiff of college was still the mandate.

Enter the NFA, and Mr. Mankopf in particular. The day after the NFL made its official announcement that no team would offer a contract to Duane Dunkle, Mr. Mankopf sent the young behemoth a telegram telling him to expect a visit from the head coach of the Cossacks. There was no mention of me in the telegram, but Lou had decided I should tag along, and here I was riding shotgun as we tooled along route 17 in his black Taurus.

It was a clear sunny day and we both wore shades. Manic gypsy chords from a Django Reinhardt CD filled the car as we drove onward in search of Chambersville, NY, pop.1247. A greasy spoon breakfast of eggs and home fries sat uneasy in my bowels, but I was otherwise content. This was a fine opportunity for me. It wasn't so much a scouting trip—everyone knew that Dunkle was a blue-chipper—as a chance for me to show that I could be part of a good recruiting team. We were supposed to schmooze the big ape.

I turned down the volume a little. The dashboard clock read 8:45, and kickoff was 11:30. These Saturday high school games started early. "What do you think, Lou, we gonna make it in time?"

Lou kept his eye on the road. "No sweat. We'll be there in half an hour. Just long enough for me to tell you about the time I ended up in the sack with Diana Rigg."

Closing my ears (for I had heard this lie before), I sat back and considered what the future might hold for me. I could see myself jetting all over the country doing this sort of thing. Alas, this trip wasn't even an over-nighter. We would see the game, meet with the young man and his folks for dinner, and then drive back to Centerport in time to catch Saturday Night Live, if we so desired.

Chambersville sat in a valley at the tip of one of the smaller Finger Lakes. The main drag was about three blocks long and lined on either side with the usual complement of small town businesses: pizza joint, mom & pop video store, old-style pharmacy, seedy-looking IGA, craft & candle shoppe, a dentist's office whose shingle bore a name from the Arabian Nights, a Volunteers of America thrift store, and a tiny white-clapboard establishment called "The Fudgery," which struck me as a terrible name for anything. We found the high school with ease and proceeded to the adjoining stadium.

Ah, the pomp of small town high school football! The racket of the marching band, the spangled, farm-fresh majorettes, the bleacher seats full of fans in school colors, and on the field the two teams running out like Homeric warriors, fully aware that it will never get any better than this.

There's no need to tell you about the game, the details of which have already passed from my memory, but this Dunkle kid was the real thing. He was so big that it seemed unfair to let him play with normal teenagers. He towered over them, and on defense threw his blockers aside like a man parting shrubbery. On offense he was a barrier of insistent flesh, protecting his quarterback from the molestations of linebackers and defensive ends. Dutifully I took notes, commenting on Dunkle's pile-driving strength and nimble footwork. Near the end of the second quarter I put my notepad in my coat pocket. There was nothing more to say.

During halftime we asked around and were pointed to Duane's rooting section, a contingent of siblings and cousins and aunts and uncles, each one massive from shoulder to shank. When we said who we were they greeted us warmly and made a space between the boy's mother and grandfather. Duane and his mom lived on grandpa's farm, dad having perished a decade earlier under an over-turned John Deere. I stared in fascination at the mother, who was a shade over five feet and didn't seem to have enough lard on her to grease a griddle. How, I wondered, had such a giant been housed in that small belly for nine months? Lou was thinking the same thing, and later that night we had quite a discussion about this wonder of nature during the ride back to Centerport.

After the game we were herded out to the family farm for a celebratory dinner. Lou protested at first, pointing out that Mr. Mankopf had made dinner reservations for the entire family at a steakhouse overlooking the lake. But the Dunkles wouldn't hear of it.

Grandma had remained at the farm to prepare Duane's favorite supper, Pork chops with cabbage and noodles, dumpling soup, and a king-sized chocolate cake with white butter-cream icing. So Lou canceled the reservations and we spent some quality time at the farm chatting with the Dunkles and hanging out in the barnyard with goats and chickens. Then Duane's pickup came up the long dirt driveway and he got out with his girlfriend Brittney, a skinny little cheerleader not unlike Ma Dunkle, and we shook hands and went inside to eat.

The table was jam-packed with good eats. Big bowls of roasted potatoes, buttered carrots, and string beans passed around family style. A steaming bowl of dumpling soup at everyone's place. Mountainous platters of pork chops and oven-hot biscuits. And that damn cake—a sheet cake so big and thick it looked like finger food for Godzilla—waiting on the sideboard. There would be fresh milk and coffee with the cake, but no beer or wine, the Dunkles being members of a local congregation that cursed the intemperate. Conversation flowed easily. These were friendly, curious people who wanted to know all about our team and Duane's prospects. Lou handled the talk of business and I chimed in now and then to describe the pleasant and invigorating life of a Cossack. From the living room came the sounds of a CD playing old Hank Williams songs. My plate was clean and I sat there in heavy-lidded contentment, listening to Lou and the others, convinced that one of Duane's cousins—plump but not half bad, in a milk-maid sort of way—was giving me the eye. No deal was struck, but the evening had been a success. The schmoozing had gone well.

By ten we were driving home on good, uncrowded roads. I felt happy. "Lou, if this is scouting, I'm for it."

He laughed at me. "You're such a baby. Tonight was pleasant, but it's not always like this. Usually it's a bad mattress in a cheap motel and a box of donuts from an all-night convenience store."

"I'll take my chances," I said. And I meant it. Given the opportunity, I would be in this for the long haul.

The next time I get serious about a woman I will make damn sure that she and I like the same kind of music. This never occurred to me when I was younger and full of juice. If a nubile nineteen-year-old, all sex-sweat and tan lines, wanted to put on Kiss or Patti Smith, fine by me. After the copulation I'd be ordering a pizza or heading home anyway. And if things were more serious, if we would actually be spending time together, I could always fall back on the "turn-down-the-music-so we can-talk" ploy. I've yet to meet a woman who would rather listen to her favorite group than talk about her feelings.

During my courtship with Annette I remember being somewhat disturbed by her taste in music. She didn't seem to have any. She listened to the radio, scanning for something with a beat so she could dance around the room. That she often did this in her panties and nothing else was one of the reasons I filed "musical interests" way back in the rear of my Annette brainfile, along with "cooking skills." She wasn't the best cook in the world and I didn't really care. We'd have plenty of takeout, and of course in time she would get better. Ditto the music. After a few years under my tutelage her George Michael tapes would be dusty and she'd be listening with pleasure to my old Cream LPs. Meanwhile let her turn on the radio and boogie across the room, her naked breasts—so taut and luscious that I weep to recall them—bouncing and bouncing in my line of sight.

But in fact after a year of marriage her lack of interest in rock groups that I considered essential started to bug me. When I played Led Zeppelin at the proper volume— loud enough to bloody the ears of an airplane spotter—she ran screaming from the room. Literally. I thought she might like Frank Zappa's *Hot Rats*. After listening for a few minutes she said, "Why would anyone write a song about a pimp?" She heard the first few chords of a Doors song and asked, "Who's this, the Adams Family?" Okay, so the Doors were a little creepy. One night I sat her down and played The Band's second album, figuring she might like it since she had an unfathomable weakness for shitkicker music, and this was perilously close to that. But she was unmoved. She liked guys in cowboy hats who sang yodely songs of heartbreak, and that wasn't The Band.

I had been brought up to love the old hippie bands from the late sixties and early seventies. I got The Mothers of Invention along with my mother's milk. My parents were freaks all the way. In photos you can see Dad wearing a tie-dye T-shirt and stovepipe hat, his long hair almost down to his waist. Mom in a peasant ensemble put together from rummage sales, kneeling with her arms around Frodo, the Frisbee-catching, ban-dana-around-the-neck-wear-ing golden re-triever, that I only remember from photos be-cause he was poisoned by a neighbor who hated hippies. They even had the classic ve-hicle—VW bus festooned with dayglo peace signs and provocative bumper stickers. I re-call my dad one time, long after he had traded in cosmic consciousness for an every-night beer buzz, shaking his head with won-der over those callow days as he told me of the many times he had been pulled over by grim State Troopers in mirrored sunglasses.

"Christ," he said, "I actually had a bumper sticker that read, 'I Brake for Hallu-cinations.' What the hell was I thinking?"

So I guess in one sense I was lucky that I could listen to music without painful memo-ries of Annette, who had not shared many of my tastes. But other reminders of my loss were all around me. Innocently driving to the store on a Saturday I would pass a wedding party, see the beaming bride and groom coming out of a church, and I would feel it in my gut. Not that I ever cared about weddings (or do now), but on the day Annette and I were married, miserable though I was in my ill-fitting tux and surrounded by members of her family, most of whom were twitterpated or just plain mean, I finally got it when I saw her coming down the aisle. She was on the arm of her father, a shabby, failed business-man, on this day already half in the bag, and even he was transformed by being in the cir-cumference of her luminous joy. How many times before that moment had I said to An-nette, "I love you"? How often had I, effusive as a schoolboy, told my bored-to-tears friends that I really loved this girl? And yet I had only been a pretender, a mouther of slogans. Now, seeing Annette like this, in what must have been the fulfillment of a girlhood dream, my heart ached for the first time with true love. I'm talking about love that wasn't all about how pretty she was or how much she pleased me with her delicate body parts. It was about how *she* felt. As she walked slowly toward the altar, her eyes were wet and shining with the expectations of heaven on earth. I felt the challenge to measure up, to be the groom of her fantasy, and it was okay, because at that instant I wanted to devote my life to taking care of her.

I suppose if I'd been more of a man I would have done just that and we'd still be married. And I don't mean a John Wayne punch-'em-in-the-mouth type. When I want to conjure the image of a real man, I remember this guy I worked with for a couple of weeks during a vacation from college. He drove a delivery truck for a beverage distributor, and his name was Johnny Stone. It sounds like the name of a private eye or gun-runner, but Johnny Stone's job was anything but glamorous. He was in the driver's seat of his truck every morning at seven, maneuvering through the snarls of city traffic, stopping at grocery stores and businesses where they stocked cases of soda pop in their lunch rooms. I was filling in for his helper, who'd been fired or injured, or possibly both, I never really found out. I was trim and muscular, a college athlete, and I figured to do the job without breaking a sweat. I was wrong.

Johnny Stone moved at a dizzying pace. "I hope you're a hard worker," he said as we gulped down coffee and Danish at the counter of a small diner. He had a brusque manner, but it wasn't mean-spirited. It was more like, "We got a job to do, so let's fuckin' do it." Johnny was about my height, big in the shoulders and chest. He carried too much belly, but it sure as hell didn't slow him down. He had the meaty paws and thick wrists of a longshoreman, and he looked a little like Jack Warden, the film actor who often played pugs and heavy laborers.

Young and strong though I was, after the first few hours of lugging soda pop I knew I was in for a long day. Johnny had a routine. He would climb on the truck and hand cases of pop down to me and I would place them on a handcart and then turn around barely in time to snag the next one coming at me. Thing is, he didn't really *hand* the cases to me. What he did was drop one side of the case and trust me to catch it. One time I failed to do so and we had broken glass and rivers of pop on the pavement. I picked up the glass while he swore at me, and I didn't drop another one. When a handcart was full, Johnny would climb down and we would wheel it into a store or the break room of a factory. I'm pretty sure they had plastic cases by then, but Johnny's distributor was too cheap to replace the heavy ones made of wood and metal, probably left over since the days of straw hats and handlebar mustaches. After dropping off the full cases we would cart the empty ones out to the truck, and since they were so much lighter, Johnny figured it would be a snap for me to *throw* them up to him at his perch on top of the truck. This I did, and after one day on the job most of the muscles in my upper body were throbbing.

And what did Johnny Stone do every day after he drove the truck back to the lot? He went home where his wife had a quick supper waiting for him. Then he'd kiss his kids and go off to his second job, pumping gas at a Texaco station.

My stint on the soda pop truck ended when they found a full-timer to do the job. I almost wept for joy at being turned loose from the "torture truck," as I had begun describing it to my friends. But I missed

Johnny Stone. He was a good talker and he usually bought me lunch. We'd grab takeout at a diner and eat it in the truck with free sodas. He kept a tight schedule. I asked him how he could possibly work so hard, how he could give up all his free time. He just shrugged. "I got kids. There's all this shit they need. And I want them to have some money for college."

Johnny was rough around the edges but that didn't fool me. One of the stops on his route was a small grocer called "Cox Market," which just happened to be owned and operated by a well-known homosexual. His staff consisted of high school boys with pretty faces. A recurring prank among local kids was to write, in the dust on a friend's car, "I work at Cox Market."

Anyway, one time while I was on the job this Mr. Cox had a mild dispute with Johnny. They settled it quickly, but as we were leaving there were smiles and snickers from Mr. Cox and his prancing help. "Goddamn fuckin' queer," said Johnny, loud enough to be heard as we walked out the door. In the cab of the truck, however, he turned thoughtful. "That's gotta be tough, never getting married, not

119

having any kids. Having assholes like me call you queer."

To look at Johnny Stone in his rumpled, sweaty gray uniform, burnished jowly face, tendons rippling in his Popeye forearms, you might think "fag-basher." But in addition to a work ethic and a moral code, he had a heart. He was all man, if I can get away with saying that.

And that's how I should have been with Annette. Work long hard hours, put food on the table for the little ones we would have, give her an earnest boff a couple of times a week, endure the sniping of her family. It would have been worth it.

During the first year of our marriage I noticed Annette was squinting a lot, usually when trying to make out something in the distance. I suggested a visit to an optometrist, and after much caviling she gave in. They declared her nearsighted. A few days later we drove to the office to pick up her new glasses and it was like going to a funeral. Like all beautiful women, Annette thought she was not beautiful enough. Now she had to wear glasses, which would hide her lovely eyes and distract observers from the creamy skin of her face. She wasn't wearing the glasses as we left the office, but when we got to the car I insisted.

"Oh my god!" she cried, seeing the world in its vivid particularities for perhaps the first time since childhood. It was a summer afternoon, and her eyes feasted on the tree leaves that stood out sharply against the electric blue sky, the waves of heat shimmering above the dark macadam in the distance ahead, the lines and edges of houses, trees, road signs, all in thrilling, crisp definition. She described everything with a little-girl exuberance that made her more beautiful than ever, glasses or no glasses.

In her best moments Annette was a true flower child, embracing the natural world with open arms and a loving heart. Birds were a particular favorite. I'd never been crazy about birds myself, but living with Annette drew me deep into their feathered world. In time, birds had a special meaning for us. After our first night of lovemaking, as I slowly backed my car out of the driveway, the headlights illuminated a pine tree and we saw a small owl peering at us from within the dark foliage. You didn't see owls very often, so we thought it significant. Many months later we spent all the hours of an afternoon agonizing over a decision that would affect the course of our lives. Twilight came and we took a walk along a quiet country road, still deliberating. Finally we reached a solution. It pleased us both and we hugged each other tightly as we stood on the shoulder of the road, and at that moment a silent owl passed over our heads.

On long trips together we enjoyed seeing great blue herons standing like sentinels in shallow rivers. I would be driving along and Annette would shout, "There's another one!" Sometimes I would pull over, and she would call to it out the window in made-up bird language. But we stopped doing that when we realized how timid they were, always flying away, disturbed by us at their supper of fish and frogs. Often they were so numerous that I would barely glance out the window as I drove on. Did you see it, she would ask. Of course, I would say. Then which direction was it facing, she wanted to know. We called this the "Heron Test," and it became part of the private language we effortlessly devised, as all intimate couples will do.

We traveled to Hawk Mountain in eastern Pennsylvania, climbed high along the trail and rested on a promontory, marveling at the profusion of raptors soaring gracefully in the thermal updrafts. On another trail, some-where in the White Mountains, we startled a ruffed grouse, and it ran in front of us screaming like a woman in terror, a very un-birdlike sound that had us in stitches. Once a hummingbird was trapped in the old barn behind the house. For many minutes we tried to rescue it, coaxing it with a long-handled broom toward the barn's one window, but the hummingbird kept flying up into the eaves. Finally it found a perch and stayed there, hopeless, dying. Annette, smaller than me and more agile, climbed up among the dark, cracked timbers, heedless of possible spiders and hornets, and caught the tiny thing in her hand. We rushed outside and when she opened her fist it sat dazed for a second and then flew off, in search of life-giving nectar, we prayed.

Naturally Annette wanted a bird of her own, one she wouldn't have to see flying away forever. I was adamantly against it. I didn't want screeching in the house, dander in the air, bird-doo all over the place. Just a little parakeet, she said. No trouble at all, and she would do all the work. A bird in a cage puts heaven in a rage, I said, mangling William Blake, one of the poets I could remember from the class we had taken together in college. But I eventually caved in, as I usually did when she wanted something. So she got a female parakeet, yellow with green highlights, and named it Ramona. Annette tamed her, got her used to perching on fingers, and then turned her loose in the house, which had high ceilings and a wide staircase, a paradise, she figured, for a small indoor bird. I wasn't crazy about this madly fluttering thing coming toward my head and then veering off at the last minute with an admonitory screech. Nor did I appreciate the deposits of parakeet guano on the arm of my easy chair, even though they were only the size of peppercorns. But one chilly night while Annette and I sat on the couch watching the tube, Ramona decided to burrow into the hollow created by the flannel shirt I had left open at the top button. She hunched down to get warm, her soft downy head mere inches from my chin, her eyes slowly closing, and I was hooked.

The next morning Annette found her dead in the cage, lying on her side, her little claw feet tightly curled. In tears, Annette said she had noticed Ramona pecking at the paint chips gathered on the window sills. It was an old house with lead paint still on the moldings. We didn't get another bird after that.

How bad a husband could I have been? During most of our marriage I was not a drunk. I didn't beat her, nor did I actively suppress her desire to stretch her wings. When she mused over the possibility of going to graduate school, I instantly saw her swooning over some dynamic prof with a seductive rap and lots of facial hair, or doing all-nighters with a male study partner who would of course have more than book learning on his mind. Regardless, I said sure, go ahead. I even offered to see if the company I worked for at the time would contribute to a spouse's continuing education. But it never came to that. Her idea had been to get an MFA in photography, and she thought she had a great idea: a series of photographs showing the deplorable conditions some people allow their properties to fall into. Crumbling shacks you see by the side of the road, the front yards littered with old tires, a rotting mattress, broken toys, refrigerator without a door. And on the front porch a shirtless country boy in jeans and cowboy boots, tattooed, unshaven, drinking beer while off to the side of the house a brood of half-naked barefoot filthy urchins use pointed sticks to torment a chained-up dog. She hoped to develop this project into a book called *American Squalor.* I said why not just do the book and forget the MFA? She bristled at that. Said I was trying to control her. I countered by suggesting that the whole idea was rather mean-spirited anyway, making fun of poor white trash that way. It grew into a pretty bad fight, but I especially remember it because it was the first time Annette brought up the idea that I was a controlling husband.

I dove into the marriage like young Lochinvar, my intentions noble and romantic. But like many immature husbands I became insensitive, selfish, a boor. It made perfect sense to me that a televised football game was more important than a family reunion (her side—mine didn't *have* reunions), and if compelled to forgo the game for the reunion, I would mope and complain the whole time. I cared little about her friends, her interests, even, I am ashamed to admit, her deepest thoughts. I would grow attentive only when angling for a carnal payoff. No wonder she left me.

And was Annette the perfect wife? Pretty close. If I may be allowed an ungentlemanly lapse, I will say that she could be a tad judgmental. In the abstract realm she had a great love for humanity, but she couldn't hold her tongue when she saw some fat guy waddling down the pavement. "Good lord," she'd say, from the ease and privilege of the air-conditioned company car I was driving, "look at that fat slob! Where's his self-respect? Something should be done about people like that." Like what? I might wonder aloud. Forced interment at a fat farm? But then she would turn her wrath on me, so usually I left my thoughts unvoiced. In supermarkets I would get nervous if we stood in line behind some blimp whose cart was filled with pillow-sized packages of cheese doodles and half-gallon tubs of ice cream. Annette would sneer and glower and cluck her tongue. I was always waiting for that one time when she would go over the edge and begin a diatribe against fat pigs who couldn't control their appetites. I read an article once about this actress—I think it was the one who played the catty neighbor on *The Mary Tyler Moore Show*—who considered it her mission in life to publicly chastise fatties for their poor food choices. In fear, I disposed of the article before Annette could see it. But I needn't have worried. She was too refined to get into a shouting match with some fatso in a public place.

Annette had an iron will and the metabolism of a ferret. She would occasionally gorge on fried chicken dinners and hot fudge sundaes, but never gained an ounce because for days afterward she would devote herself to aerobic self-punishment and leafy salads. She never smoked a cigarette in her life and so could not understand the kind of weakness that allowed a person to foul her lungs and stink up her clothes with sediments of a poisonous drug, as did my cheerfully unapologetic mother. Studious as a monk, she had been mostly an A student all her life and planned to go back to school after raising the two children we would produce. But I feared for those children, saw them condemned to marathons of homework, to dancing or music lessons on Saturday mornings when they should be out playing. Of course we never had any.

Annette was a classic type-A personality, tightly-strung, highly driven, impatient, snappish. I'm the sort who daydreams of lying in a hammock on a south sea island, eating orange slices while bare-breasted native girls fan me with palm leaves. How we managed to stay together as long as we did is less of a mystery when you consider that she must have seen in me an antidote to her tensions and strivings. Sometimes it would work. Relax, I'd say, wrapping my arm around her waist and gently pulling her away from the countertop where she was angrily writing down points to bring up during her next phone argument with her sister. I would draw her into the living room and force her into a chair, and then give her a couple of options for something fun to do, right now, at that very moment. On one such occasion I drove us to the local tennis courts and we swatted balls back and forth for an hour. It was August and muggy, and we were sweat-drenched and loving it. She was inexperienced at tennis but a natural; I had recently taught her the rudiments of the forehand and backhand strokes, and on this day we were able to have good long rallies. The courts were high on a hill and we stopped a couple of times to watch a distant display of weird orange lightning streaks confined within a raft of gigantic cumulous clouds, the kind that fill the sky all the way to the top, like a mountain range. So far off were they that the rumbles of thunder were soft echoes. Toward the end of our rallying, after an especially long and satisfying exchange, Annette ran to the net and beckoned me forward, her smile wide, her forehead beaded with sweat, her eyes bright with joy. When I got there she pulled me close and gave me a sweaty kiss. "I love you!" she cried, backpedaling to her position on the court, and it was one of those moments when your life swells up with the warmth and volume of pure happiness, and all your pains are reduced to mouse droppings in a corner of the basement.

When things get really bad, when I miss her with a palpable ache in my chest, I try to think of her family. That usually makes it better. Her sister I've already mentioned, but let me go into some detail here. First of all, she was a knockout. Annette was the classic girl next door, lovely and appealing in a sweet-faced, slender way. Karen was Playboy Bunny material, with womanly hips and breasts, elegant limbs, the florid face of a starlet. I was already in love with Annette and completely satisfied with her sexually, but the first time I saw Karen—in a yellow bikini, poolside, nut brown and glistening with sweat and sun tan oil—I found myself wondering if it would ever be possible to get both of them into my bed at the same time. Alas, after just a couple of days spent in her company at the family estate in Vermont, I realized that Karen had the personality of a wolverine with a migraine, and there went the hot fantasy, because I'm not so hard up that I would want sex without at least the semblance of congeniality.

Karen's problem, as I saw it, was old-time religion, an especially virulent strain of godliness that I thought only occurred in the deep South. But here it was in the North country, fueled by old money, small town intolerance, and her churchy parents—her dad a simpering, mousy fellow who had a secret stash of fruited brandy in the basement, her mom a broad-shouldered battleaxe who ran the household with the *cojones* of a Mexican warlord.

Now I have some strong opinions about religion, which has been stalking me for years, nipping at my ankles like a grouchy little mutt. Hippie pals doing one trip too many and finding the Lord. A beautiful woman I follow out of a store and into a parking lot until she leads me to a car with a bumper sticker that says "Honk if you love Jesus." End-time potboilers taking up space on library shelves. All those bozos on TV with their gleaming rings and hideous suits peddling salvation to gullible grandmaws.

Centerport has plenty of churches, Christian bookstores, Walls painted with pro-Christian graffiti, and there's even an establishment—I'm not kidding—called "Holy Spirit Car Wash." Now this annoys the hell out of me, business types cashing in on peoples' faith. And what do those poor customers think, that if they take their cars into this godly car wash tongues of fire will descend to burn the pigeon shit off their windshields? Sometimes I feel like driving in there and cheerfully asking for the works, explaining that my car needs to look nice when I pick up the teenage hookers I've booked for the night.

Before our family fell apart I did time in a Catholic School. It wasn't terrible, but I remember being disturbed by all the emphasis on pain and suffering. During Lent, for example, we had to meet in church once a week after school for the Stations of the Cross, a ritual that could have been dreamed up by Stephen King. In the pews, kneeling or standing at the command of a clicker-crazy nun, we would follow the Monsignor as he and his cluster of acolytes prowled the aisles, stopping at each of the fourteen friezes that depicted the various torments of Jesus on the day of his crucifixion. The Monsignor would read a vivid description, usually beginning with a phrase like "Consider the incredible torment our Lord must have felt as he..." and so forth. Then he would lead the congregation in prayer, the acolytes would swing the incense burner, and it was on to the next station for more blood and guts. You had to pay attention and not fool around because one of the Jesuits would pace up and down the center aisle, his tense face a white blotch of hate, his fists balled with the fury of things held in for years, and you knew he was itching to whale on some kid who giggled or fucked up. Then they'd finish the deal with a hymn that began, "By the blood that flowed from Thee, in Thy bitter agony..." This was the only church activity I didn't mind. It was like being at a horror movie.

To Annette's family I was one dog-sacrifice away from being a priest in the Church of Satan. Foolishly, I did nothing to change their bad opinion of me. During one of sister Karen's visits I walked through the TV room as she and Annette were watching a nice religious flick, *The Song of Bernadette.* I paused for a moment as I caught sight of Vincent Price on the screen. "Hey," I said, "it's Vincent!" I stood and watched the scene for a moment. He was playing some sort of town councilman or business leader or something. I walked away, saying, "I liked him better as The Abominable Dr. Phibes." I couldn't even let them enjoy their movie without injecting something dark and sinister.

We roared into Syracuse to play the Berserkers, and absolutely crushed them, 63-17. It was a breakout game for Drew Danielson, who passed for five touchdowns and over three hundred yards before Lou rested him halfway through the third period. Mike Ponsonby took his place in a credible fashion. I was inserted into the offense and caught three passes, including my first score of the season, an eight-yard bullet that I grabbed while falling to my knees in the end zone. In the NFL it's considered poor grace to run up the score like that. But in lesser leagues there's an understanding. Players have to show their stuff.

Back in Centerport, I went with Paul Facemeyer and Bobby Hertzig to an IHOP. Thursdays meant no practice, late sleeping, and a leisurely breakfast someplace other than the dining hall. With the zeal one would expect from a 310-pound offensive tackle, Paul dove into his platter of buttermilk pancakes, home fries, bacon, and fried eggs, ignoring anything not related to food. The only

135

thing he said during the meal was, "You got any syrup over there?" He'd already drained a pitcher of maple syrup and wanted to try the blueberry I was pouring over my French toast. Bobby Hertzig, however, was quite talkative.

It so happens that I have no problem whatsoever with a gay football player. Some of the Cossacks make snide comments about him when he isn't around, and of course they razz the hell out of him to his face, which he expects. But on the whole, nobody really minds that he tip-toes through the tulips, as they say. He's a smart player who hits hard, and we're all happy to have him as a team-mate. One time Hollis Daft gave him a pamphlet describing a method for curing homosexuality through prayerful interaction with Jesus. Bobby read the thing and then engaged Hollis in a good-natured locker room debate that everyone stood around chuckling at. As Bobby understood it, Christians regarded homosexuality as a choice, not an accident of birth. If this is true, he said, it logically follows that any straight guy can make the choice to switch from rug-munching to dick-nibbling. Born-agains should consider the implications, he continued, and pray double-time to keep Satan's mustachioed, slim-waisted incubi from dawdling in their dreams. It wasn't much of a debate, actually, as Hollis dropped out rather quickly, made uncomfortable, I would guess, by the stirring of certain echoes.

What Bobby felt talkative about on this day was his broken heart. He'd fallen hard for James Veltry, but after a brief and intense affair, Veltry had dumped him. Those players on the team who paid attention to such things thought it was a shame, since they made a handsome couple. I knew that the idea of two football players having homosexual relations would have been shocking four or five years ago. But in these liberated times, and under Lou's laissez faire coaching style, few of the Cossacks seemed to care who was doing what with whom. One time in practice Veltry caught a pass and Bobby tried to bring him down but was dragged a few feet ahead with his arms around Veltry's waist and his head burrowed in his crotch. Sal Gargano yelled at him. "Come on, goddammit! You're supposed to tackle him, not suck his dick."

Somebody said something in Gargano's ear. "Oh yeah," he said, "I forgot. Never mind."

The problem was that Veltry wanted to play the field. Even though Centerport is a medium-sized city in the nowhere land of up-state New York, its gay population was on the rise at that time. A good-looking guy like James Veltry could score easily in the city's one gay bar, and he didn't want to give up that option.

Bobby sighed. "It hurts. Sooner or later a girl wants to settle down."

I had to agree. The serial heartbreaks of the single life could break a man's spirit. "Don't worry, Bobby. You'll find someone. There's a girl—or in your case, a guy—out there for each of us."

Paul Facemeyer reached across the table and used his fork to spear the last sausage link on my plate. "I can't stand to see food go to waste," he said, before shoving the link into his mouth.

"Jeez, Paul," said Bobby, "you might have asked first. Maybe Fin was planning to eat that sausage."

Facemeyer shrugged. "Who cares," he said, chewing contentedly. "Man's gotta take what he wants in this life."

After we settled the bill, I took the fellas back to the dorm and drove onward to a large pier that overlooked the lake at Centerport's east end. I liked coming to the pier to feed the ducks and the seagulls, and I kept a bag of bread in my car for just that purpose. It was a fine autumn day and I stood at the edge of the pier tossing crumbles of bread into the water. The ducks didn't seem very hungry— some of them even refused to swim over to the floating pieces—but a handful of seagulls in attendance made enough ruckus for an entire aviary. They preferred to feed on the pier, and in the air. I threw bread chunks up high and marveled at the gulls' ability to feed on the fly, snatching the morsels like a first-baseman gloving a throw from the shortstop. When the bread ran out I wiped my hands on my jeans and sat down on a bench. Gradually the gulls took their leave, save for one who stood a few feet away, staring at me with a scathing eye. "Sorry, dude," I said. "I'm all out." I displayed my empty hands and the gull, frightened by the gesture, flew away.

I sat in the piercing afternoon sun and looked out at the lake, at the diamond-light shifting and shimmering on the gentle waves. Close by, two mated ducks paddled in the water without much ambition, apparently just enjoying the day. A white-haired old man, his granddaughter's hand in his, strolled past me to the end of the pier. The little girl peppered him with questions and commentary in an unselfconsciously loud voice.

A restless feeling took hold of me and I got in my car and drove around for a while. I did this until chance took me past an old theater that was showing a matinee double feature. I parked and bought a ticket and seated myself in the cavernous dark as the first movie was ending. I watched spectacular special effects showing the destruction of an entire planet while the crew of an escaping space ship barked vile profanities at each other. The second feature was set in contemporary Los Angeles and opened with a long car chase culminating in the obliteration of an open-air café. The action was non-stop—bloody fistfights, graphic sexual encounters, men shooting at each other in a shopping mall—but my eyelids grew heavy and I drifted in and out of unsatisfying catnaps. I left before the movie ended, rather than watch a scene in which the bare-chested hero was about to be tortured by Chinese gangsters with cattle prods.

Cool dusk had settled upon Centerport. I drove to a family-style restaurant and consumed a dinner of meatloaf, mashed potatoes, gravy and corn niblets. I dawdled over my meal, glancing up now and then to watch my fellow diners gabbing to each other as they tucked into their meals.

I returned to the dorm a little before nine, very tired and a little sad. My mood was not improved by what I found. Guy Smeeks and Chunky Hanrahan were having a contest to see who could piss the farthest. The problem was that they were having this contest in the hallway, not far from my room. There had been other contestants, and the air was heavy with the stink of urine.

"Christ almighty," I said, "What the hell's wrong with you guys? Can't you do this in the bathroom, or out on the lawn?"

"Chill out, Fin," said Kilmer Joyce. He had a tape measure and a clipboard, was obviously the score keeper. "I got everything under control." He pointed to a clothes basket filled with towels, presumably for mopping up. By tip-toeing and squinching close to the wall, I avoided the puddles and made it to my room. I slammed the door and wadded a towel under the crack to keep out the flooding piss. For the next half-hour I lay in bed listening to the shouting and arguing in the hallway, until I heard Sal Gargano's disgusted voice telling everyone to clean up the goddamn mess and go to their rooms.

Before falling asleep, I decided it was foolish to wait any longer. Tomorrow I would call Laura and ask her out for the weekend.

It turned out to be a simple matter. I made the call, and after a brief exchange of small talk suggested we have dinner on Saturday night. To my relief, she agreed. I said that since she knew the town better than I did, she could choose the restaurant. She chose the Cadillac Diner and said she'd meet me at six.

After hanging up, I started to worry. A *diner?* I should have suggested someplace fancy. Would she think me a piker? Maybe she was waiting for me to take charge and say forget the diner, let's find a French restaurant and sup on lark tongues and truffles. Maybe I should call her back right away. And what was that about meeting me there? She didn't want me to pick her up at her house, didn't want me to know her address? What did she think, I was a stalker? And by driving to the diner herself, she could take off whenever she wanted if my company became unbearable. What about her son? She had not mentioned him. Should I have said, "Bring Cody"? Would she bring him anyway, as a means to prevent me from reaching across the table and grabbing her tits?

That's what I don't like about dating. It's a game, but the rules are unacknowledged and often concealed. I've heard girls say, "Oh, I date a lot of guys. It's fun. I like to get out and do things." This always irritates me. You want to get out and do things, take your girlfriend. Real dating is a serious business for both parties. The girl is sizing the guy up as a potential lifemate even as he's scheming ways to get her hand on his dick. She wants to find out if he'll spend his money on her without complaining about it every other minute, whether he can carry a conversation that isn't about beer and pro wresting, whether he can eat a Chinese dinner without getting duck sauce on his forehead. Is he presentable, marriageable? And of course sometimes the roles are reversed. Some guys are sensitive, looking for more than a hole and a heartbeat. And some girls are horny as a castaway on an oyster diet.

I think it was a lot easier back in the late sixties. In those days, apparently, people would meet and if they liked what they saw they'd be doing it a couple of hours later. That's how my parents hooked up, tripping their brains out at some music fest in Maine when they bumped into each other and ended up balling (which is what they called it back then) under a tree. A week later they were living together in a commune. Within a year they got married because it was a way to get money from the relatives. By the time my siblings and I were in the picture, Mom was studying Eckankar (and I still don't know what the hell *that* was about) and Dad had given up tripping for good old-fashioned booze.

Well, I was thinking too much. I had to stop over-complicating things. Just kick back and enjoy the date.

The Cadillac Diner was so named because it had a red Cadillac on the roof. The place was all chrome and neon, and the waitresses wore uniforms and little hats reminiscent of old car-hops. Laura and I both ordered the burger and fries platter, with milk shakes. What else would you order at a fifties-style diner? The burger was succulent, with the roll lightly toasted the way it gets when the fry cook presses it down on the grill for a few seconds with a big metal spatula. Too often I have been served a burger on a huge, dried-out hard roll. Don't people know that a burger needs to be served on a regular old bun? And to do it right, there should even be some grease on the top, so you can feel it under your fingers when you grab hold of it. But the Cadillac Diner knew how to put together a hamburg platter. The fries were cut from fresh potatoes; they weren't those bleached twigs that rattle around frozen in plastic packages. And the milk shake was good and thick, but not so thick you couldn't suck it up through your straw. It was made with a superior brand of dark chocolate ice cream, and this made me think of my brother Kevin, a great connoisseur of chocolate. One time in a luncheonette Kevin told the waitress to make his chocolate shake "as dark and rich as the thighs of a Nigerian harlot." As I recall, the waitress said, "'kay," and went about her business.

It seems I share with Kevin a love of chocolate, and also an urge to charm with words, although my younger brother is much more accomplished in that department. It's an Irish thing, according to our Grandfather, who told us this one night when we were barely teenagers. "You boys come from a long line of raconteurs," he said. "Fine men who preferred spending their time in pubs entertaining fellas with yarns, rather than sit home by the hearth with the wife and kids." He paused, smiling wistfully. "God love us for Irishmen."

Now that I'm older, I reject the idea that a man can find more pleasure in a bar than at home, but I was happy to believe that at least I would never be tongue-tied. And in fact I was delightfully glib during the first few minutes of this date with Laura, while we chatted and surveyed the surroundings. Then the food came and we proceeded to the next level. A date, after all, consists in gradual revelations of character. One's approach to food is often an indicator of carnal attitudes. It pleased me to see Laura pick up the burger and take a nice healthy bite, heedless of any concern that her lusty mastication of beef might be considered unladylike. On the other hand, she wasn't tearing into it like a wild dog, flashing her incisors and grunting as hot blood and grilled onions dribbled down her chin. Such a performance would have suggested an over-physical and indelicate sexuality, just as tiny nibbles and incessant napkin dabbing could mean frigidity.

I wondered if Laura was watching my eating habits as well, and drawing similar conclusions. I didn't care. I ate naturally, but not disgustingly. I would be deemed acceptable. Furtively I licked the ketchup off the rim of my hamburger bun so it wouldn't end up all over my mouth. I wanted to look my best. Friday afternoon I'd gotten a haircut, after asking Lou if I should. Why not, said Lou, adding it didn't much matter since I was on course to becoming a bald guy. How would you know, I said, adding that at his height the only hair Lou ever saw was around my crotch. I still have plenty of hair, by the way, but I *am* starting to recede a little in front. It bothers me, but not too much. My father was bald by his late forties, and he never lacked for female companionship. He spent the last year of his life shacked-up with an exotic dancer. She didn't seem to mind that he had a bald head, booze burns all over his face, and a fat stomach. Women, god bless them, tend to overlook such imperfections.

"Cody's excited about going to the game," said Laura. "After you gave me the tickets and I thought about it, I almost didn't tell him, because you play on a school night. But then I saw that it starts at seven."

"Right," I said. "We're not like the NFL, or baseball. We actually *want* kids to see us play."

The NFA had gotten a lot of good press because of their early kickoffs. It would be nice if our example could rub off on other pro leagues, but I'm not holding my breath. It seems to me that the corporations who pay for commercial time during sports broadcasts don't care about kids, because kids aren't the ones buying SUVs and mutual funds. But it's not just the corporations. None of the owners or athletes cares, either. You never hear any of them take up for kids who can't watch the seventh game of a World Series because it's on too late. All they talk about is money, and how they're not making enough of it. Yet I don't expect a single one of them will end up living in a cardboard box somewhere.

"Where *is* Cody?" I asked. "You get a sitter?"

"I dropped him off at my sister's," said Laura. "She has two kids Cody's age and a big-screen TV. I'll have to drag him away."

We were too stuffed to order dessert, so I walked her to her car. It was a beautiful night, the clear blue sky gradually darkening over a scarlet rim of sunset. I opened the door for her, and she paused a moment and turned to face me, just long enough so I could lean forward and kiss her on the lips. She returned the kiss, and smiled, and got into her car and drove away.

When I was thirteen and being hammered by puberty, my older sister Debbie saw what I was going through and took pity on me. She was a frank person even back then, when she was seventeen, and so felt no embarrassment in asking me one sweaty summer night if I'd started pulling my pud yet. I told her to fuck off, but she persisted.

"You're an idiot," she said. "You act tough but you don't know anything. I can help you."

I hated to admit it, but she was right. I wasn't about to open up to her about my masturbatory habits, which had been going full-throttle for almost a year, but I was ready to listen. Debbie was considered worldly by all her friends. She was going out with a college guy in his twenties, and she often spent weekends at his apartment. Dad was gone from the family by then, moved out on his own to pursue his drinking and whoring, and mom was so whacked out on pot and her screwy religion that she took little notice of what was going on with her own kids. Among the conflicts tormenting me that summer was my attraction to my own sister. Debbie was a cute girl with strawberry blonde hair and freckles around her nose and a lithe swimmer's body. I dealt with the attraction by being surly to her. But on this occasion I paid attention.

For the next hour or so she gave me the scoop on female sexuality. Some of the stuff I was already dimly aware of, but there was enough new information of an alarming nature to take the top of my head off. I tried to look casual, but my palms and armpits had grown damp.

When she was done, Debbie said, "Look, you're not going to be *using* any of this information for quite a while—

"How do *you* know?" I interrupted, a debonair rake.

She laughed in my face. "Trust me, kid, I know. And as I was saying, before you cut me off, you should at least know the proper way to kiss a girl."

She said most guys don't have a clue, and think you're supposed to shove your big sluggy tongue into a girl's mouth and slobber all over her. She said to take it slow, and be gentle, and that my tongue should be more like a guppy nibbling at the glass of its aquarium.

I never forgot that advice, and it had worked well for me, except for a few occasions with ardent lovers who had made fun of my wimpy, hesitant tongue. On this first date with Laura, I didn't even unleash the guppy. My kiss was a respectful, dry affair of the lips only, and she seemed to appreciate it. When I returned to the dorm I got right into bed and indulged impure thoughts about Laura Barnett. I loved her face and her eyes. I imagined what those lovely green eyes would look like as pleasure widened their pupils. On our date she had worn a light blue satin blouse, and I visualized slowly unbuttoning it and reaching in to feel her breasts and to brush my fingertips across her hard nipples.

I completed my solitary business and lay relaxed for a minute. It wasn't a minute too soon. Out in the hallway there was a commotion. Offensive left tackle Klaus Kohler was marching along singing one of his beer hall songs in a voice so loud they could probably hear him in Dusseldorf, where I wished he would go back to immediately. His compatriots of the evening, whoever they were, shouted and laughed, egging him on. They

152

were banging on doors, too. Fortunately mine was locked.

I was too old for this shit.

When I was a kid I never had a best friend and I can't really say that I have one now. I like it that way, because there are moments when one of my friends will do something that makes me realize he *is* a best friend, and then he recedes into the background when some other friend does something equally wonderful. Case in point is a buddy of mine named Joe Ludka, who I mention now because he came to visit me in Centerport during the week we were preparing to play the Manchester Purple Demons.

The first time I met Joe I thought he was a jerk. We were at Camp Catawba together—Lou had recruited him to teach basketball—and I came into a cabin where Joe was resting on a bunk jawing with some other counselors. Lou made the introductions and I shook hands with the other guys, but when I moved toward Joe he remained supine on the bunk and extended his leg, offering me his bare foot to grasp. I declined of course, amid general laughter, and would have thought it a

153

normal jest but for the fact that Joe put his leg back and went on with his conversation as if I had never entered the room.

The next time I saw him it was dusk and he was heading out for a night on the town. He greeted me in a friendly, almost exuberant way, but I was fixated on the canary yellow V-neck sweater he wore. What a doofus, I thought.

But this was a classic case of a bad first impression, because within two or three days I realized that Joe Ludka and I would be pals for life. Joe was a rangy six-three, but in his youth he had been, by his own admission, a fat kid, so he carried some residual thickness that now, in his prime, hung on his bones as muscle. He was Latvian and had a Latvian skull. I had never known what a Latvian skull was until Joe told me that's what he had. It was long and equine, with prominent teeth that seemed always displayed in amusement. He was good-looking in a goofy way, but one of the wise guys at camp told him he looked like Arnold Schwarzenegger after reconstructive head surgery, and I could kind of see it.

Joe and I were only a couple of years apart and had absorbed the same quantity of popular culture and had several thousand things in common. His observations were penetrating. One morning in the dining hall as the conversation turned to sidekicks in old westerns, he remarked that Andy Devine had the remarkable quality of being able to project a strong sense of B.O. in a medium that lacked an olfactory dimension. Those of us who had seen the film work of Andy Devine—unshaven, greasy, huge in the belly and undoubtedly foul in the trousers—were suddenly in awe of Joe Ludka.

I later learned that Joe had low blood sugar and a variety of other ailments, some of them psychosomatic, that would zone him out as the day wore on. He had been in one of his zones on the night I thought he was dissing me.

But the thing that really united us in friendship was our shared sense of having been done in by a woman. I was still smarting from my failed marriage, and Joe was in almost the same boat. He hadn't been married, but the sculptress he'd cohabited with for two years had found someone she liked better and dumped him without warning. So he and I felt the same kind of pain.

Now it is common for a man with a broken heart to do a lot of crying in his beer and sometimes get so drunk that he will start an ill-advised fistfight or drive his car into a ditch, all in the name of lost love. And I have certainly been known to do those kinds of things. But Joe was a stabilizing influence. He had enough pain, he said, without adding on the misery of the drinking experience. So what we did on our nights off was go into the sleepy town five miles from camp and shop for necessaries like shower shoes and mosquito repellant, and then enjoy a meal at Friendly's. There, while sipping thick milkshakes which the Friendly's corporation preferred to call *frappes*, we would hash out the torments of the seduced and abandoned male. We did this so often that Friendly's became known as our personal watering hole. Counselors would bring a troop of kids in after a movie or a round of miniature golf and see us in our corner booth, the table littered with dirty napkins, sticky with frappe droppings. Sometimes they'd send over a round of frappes, as a joke, and we drank every last one. Once I looked up from the murky depths of my double chocolate frappe and saw Lou standing next to the table, a look of amused disdain on his tanned face.

"Hard to believe," he said. "Two grown men spending their nights off at an ice cream parlor. Do you realize how gay this is? Don't you know that at this very moment there are dozens of horny women perched on barstools all over town?"

I was mute, staring idiotically at Lou with half-open, chocolate-smeared lips. But Joe had a ready answer. To our favorite waitress he called, "Hey Viv, another fudge royale frappe over here, and keep 'em coming."

We grew so immersed in the place that we wrote up a list of top ten things overheard at Friendly's, and sent it in to David Letterman. Joe contributed the best line: "Waiter, there's a vole in my frappe!" But we never heard back from Letterman, the punk.

When camp ended Joe and I stayed in touch by phone, sharing stories of our romantic pursuits and failures. We agreed that our bonding experience had seemed like what two lost souls might have gone through during their first few weeks in the French Foreign Legion. Completely absurd, of course, but we bought into it, probably because some of our favorite clowns had done time in that service. I refer to The Three Stooges and Laurel & Hardy. Which reminds me of what Joe did one night to establish himself as a true blue friend.

Like all red-blooded American males I am a big fan of the Stooges, Stan and Ollie, and certain other practitioners of the slapstick arts. But my all-time favorite comedy team is Jackie Gleason, Art Carney, and Audrey Meadows in *The Honeymooners.* Alas, during the months after my term at Camp Cawtaba I was living in a small city in Ohio, where I had gone for a job that sounded good but ended badly. Depressed, broke, and unable to travel because the job had come with a company car that I no longer possessed, I was stranded in a tiny apartment in a part of the country where I had no friends. Christmas was due in a couple of days and I was feeling extremely sad for myself as I trudged back from the store with the fixings of what would be my big holiday meal: hot dogs, orange soda, and two packages of "Snowballs," which the initiated will know as crème-filled, chocolate cake balls covered in snowy white marshmallow frosting with shredded coconut.

I took these items out of the bag and wished I could at least watch something good on TV, but my cable had been shut off and all I could pick up on the regular antenna was a shaky transmission from a channel in West Virginia, which seemed always to be airing *Hee Haw* or a local square dance program. At that moment the phone rang.

It was Joe, wishing me Christmas cheer. I told him of my miseries, and he was sympathetic. I especially complained about my TV situation, and lamented that I could not watch *The Honeymooners.* Joe, calling from New York City, mentioned that by coincidence that very show was going to air in about five minutes. Well, I said, you go ahead and enjoy it, and I'll read myself to sleep with the local pennysaver. But he wouldn't hear of it. He put the phone next to the TV set and turned up the volume and told me sit back and enjoy. Joe watched it too—I could hear his staccato laughter in the background—and during commercials he would get on the phone so we could discuss the finer points of Gleason's comedic genius. This was back in the day before phone company wars, and Joe didn't have a lot of money, so it was a definite financial sacrifice for him to do this. I had said it wasn't necessary, but he insisted. And for thirty minutes I basked in the pleasure of *The Honeymooners* and the glow of good fellowship.

Now Joe was coming to visit me at Cossack headquarters, and I wanted to show him a good time.

"Don't make any special plans," he said when we spoke the night before his arrival. "I just need a day or two away from all the sturm and drang." He was referring to his job as head basketball coach for a small college in New York City, and life with his young wife, an exceptionally pretty girl who I figured was high maintenance.

"Whatever you want, Joe. We can take in a movie, hang out at the dorms, maybe play some tennis. Bring your racket."

"Sounds good," he said. "They got a Friendly's in Centerport?"

Joe arrived on Monday afternoon, just as practice was winding down. Lou greeted him warmly and they stood on the sideline chatting and watching a casual scrimmage between the offense and defense. I was on the field at the time, always eager to participate in scrimmages since I knew I wouldn't see a lot of action in real games. During a drive that had begun on our 20, I had caught three perfect spirals from Mike Ponsonby, Drew's backup and a guy who had NFL talent but some flaws that prevented him from rising to the top. He was, for example, a pathological womanizer, which kept him out past curfew and drained his vital essences. He could throw an eighty-yard spiral, a feather-soft floater, and a bullet that hurt so much it could bring tears to the eyes of a gnarly tight end. At 6'5", 230, he had the size of the pro-totypical NFL quarterback. But he had lapses in concentration, often because he was just too tired from nocturnal carousing. I enjoyed Mike and hoped he would make it big some-day. He was a charmer with long dark flowing locks and thick Mick Jaggerish lips. An an-glophile, he wore an ascot and spoke with something resembling a British accent tainted with the twang of the Nebraska plains. On this day he was in a jolly mood because of the previous night's conquest of twin redheads.

"Hey, Mike," I said, "lemme run a fly up the middle. My buddy's on the sideline and I'd like to show off for him."

"Capital idea, old man." He *was* in a jolly mood. "Put your little self behind the d-back and I'll drop one in your outstretched fingers."

I lined up and saw Phillip Woo covering the zone I would run into, which normally would have been bad news because there was no way I could sneak behind the best natural athlete on the team. But I knew that Phillip was hungry; I'd overheard him asking Del Bennett if it was true that we were having stuffed peppers for dinner. In his mind he was already carrying his tray to the buffet table. So at the snap I ran right at him, a bored look on my face. He backpedaled a little, and I saw that he was focusing more on James Veltry who was angling in front of him from the other side. When Woo stopped moving, poised to leap forward in case Veltry was the primary receiver, I darted behind him and managed to put five yards between us before he recovered. The play had started on the 40, and now I was at the 20 and in full gear. I heard Woo yell *"Shit!"* and then I looked over

162

my shoulder and saw an absolutely beautiful Ponsonby special nosediving toward a spot a few feet in front of me. I stretched out my arms and the ball landed in my open palms uncannily soft and light, like a giant marzipan Easter egg. Woo could have dived and tripped me up at the 10, but this was practice, after all, so he just slowed to an irritated trot and let me prance into the end zone. There were hoots and hollers from the offense and then Lou blew the whistle to end practice.

After a shower I took Joe to the refectory, where stuffed peppers were indeed the highlight of the buffet. We loaded up our trays and sat at the coach's table. Joe already knew running backs coach Ellis Barry from a sports banquet in New York, and Lou introduced him to the others. As I expected, Joe entered seamlessly into the discussion already started, about athletes who had played more than one professional sport, or who could have if they'd tried. The obvious names were tossed around—Michael Jordan, Bo Jackson, Deion Sanders, Danny Ainge—and then some of the older coaches like Lou and Sal spoke of their contemporaries—Bob Gibson, Jackie Jensen, Gene Conley, Dave De-Busschere. Soon we were into trivia and obscurities. Who, asked Hollis Daft, was the only athlete ever drafted in four pro sports, soccer being the fourth. Joe (I was proud of the boy) gave the answer at once: Dave Winfield. What two-sport star had the distinction of being the only player ever to pinch hit for Ted Williams? I knew this one, thanks to my dad's collection of old baseball cards, the backs of which often gave such fascinating bits of information. The answer was Carroll Hardy, who played outfield for the Red Sox and halfback for Colorado. (Since Hardy was a lifetime .240 hitter, one assumes that Ted Williams had to be taken out of the game because of an injury.) And on it went. Athletes turned actors: Jim Brown, Fred Dryer, Ed Marinaro. Actors who had played ball in college: John Wayne, Dan Blocker, Dean Cain, Woody Strode. A discussion began about which pro tennis players might have the natural talent to play baseball. Tom Paterson said that John McEnroe and Jimmy Connors, with their lateral quickness and soft hands, would have made a terrific double play combo. Lou pointed out that both were left handed, so he put Connors at first base and had McEnroe in right field. "Michael Chang at second," he said, "and Federer at short."

"What about third base?" asked Patterson.

"Agassi," said Lou. "Fast hands, strong arm."

After long debate we had Boris Becker in left, Borg in center, and Pete Sampras on the mound, on the theory that a cannonball serve requires for its completion the same biomechanical pattern as a high hard one. We were stumped over who should catch, until Lou suggested an obscure South African pro named Johan Kriek, the only tennis player anyone could think of who had the stocky, muscular body type needed for the blocking of home plate.

Then it was time to wonder if any baseball players had played tennis.

"Larry Gura," said Sal.

"He was good?" I asked.

"I don't know how good he was, but I know he played. That's how come he got traded from the Yankees to Kansas City. Billy Martin found out Gura was a tennis player so he traded him. Martin thought tennis was a pussy sport."

I told the group that speaking of tennis it was time for Joe and I to leave. We had agreed to play a match against David Kanogo and Phillip Woo, and wanted a few moments to relax first. As we left the dining hall, Joe said, "Look how we spend all our time. Playing sports, coaching sports, talking about sports. Meanwhile other men are inspecting bridges or performing neurosurgery."

I couldn't argue with him. Like the old sportswriter Jimmy Cannon once said, I work in the toy department.

For the next hour we sat on a veranda outside the dining hall, catching each other up on our respective lives, and lazily watching the foot-traffic on the generously lawned and leafy campus. Although the prep school was no more, Mr. Mankopf, not one to waste good real estate, periodically rented dorm rooms and the rest of the facilities to various groups for two or three week stays. At this time some sort of wrestling camp was underway, and all day long we would see high schoolers in sweat-soaked T-shirts and gym trunks heading in small clumps from station to station. A trio of boisterous, incredibly fit teenagers passed a few feet from where Joe and I sat and waved at us. These kids admired the Cossacks, professional athletes who occupied a niche they someday hoped to reach. We waved back. It was nice to see these youngsters working hard at a sport, but to be honest I have always had a queasy feeling about wrestling. Rolling around on a mat with a sweaty male is not my idea of a good time.

A sudden thought occurred to me. "Why couldn't this be cheerleading camp?"

"Boy, wouldn't that be nice," said Joe. "Seventeen-year-old girls ripening before your eyes in an idyllic setting."

We fell quiet for a moment, imagining such splendor.

"What happened to the prep school, anyway?" asked Joe.

"Generally bad management," I said. "And a civil suit that was the final straw. Remember the spanking scandal?"

Joe's horse face contorted in a grimace of memory recall. Then he brightened. "Yes! That was here?"

I gave Joe the whole story, as I had heard it recently from Sal Gargano. Sal likes to tell the story as often as he can find a listener who is ignorant of the facts. I'm not sure why Sal is so interested. Someday I'll have to ask him. Anyway, what happened is that the school gym teacher, not ordinarily known as a disciplinarian, suddenly decided to inflict spankings on all student miscreants. But since corporal punishment was *verboten* at the school, he gave it a bizarre twist—the spanking would be administered to *him*, as a sample of what the lads could expect if they ever found themselves in a school where hands-on punishment *was* allowed. Since the ritual spanking of a gym teacher was an unusual treat, the kids were often lining up half-a-dozen deep after school to take part. The gym teacher was apparently satisfied with just being spanked, so although he was fired, no criminal charges were brought against him. But it pretty much did in the school.

Having fully digested our meal, Joe and I ambled to the tennis courts for our match with Kanogo and Woo. They were two hard courts perfectly situated at the north end of campus, which, bordering a large farm, was quiet and rustic. Pine trees blocked the setting sun, and green plastic wind barriers hung on the chain link fence. Despite the attractive milieu, our opponents were the only ones there.

Watching them hit practice rallies, I realized we were in for a rough time. David Kanogo, at 6'3", 250, was not built along the lines of a classic tennis player. Nor did he have the smooth and graceful strokes of someone who had taken lessons at an early age. His game consisted mostly of the cut and the jab, the former a sharp downward stroke that conveyed a nasty underspin to the ball, the latter a halting punch more like a volley than a full swing, which transformed the fuzzy yellow orb into a flat, brutal projectile. He was murder at the net, using his height and long arms to spear overheads, and his surprising agility to protect the alleys. A Nigerian by birth whose parents had moved their family to California when he was twelve, Kanogo was very dark with gleaming white teeth and a sly sense of humor that manifested itself in practical jokes, often of a physically painful nature. He'd been a second stringer at Fresno State, but was still developing his skills and hoped to move on to the NFL.

Phillip Woo, the most gifted athlete on the Cossacks, had been raised in the suburbs of Auckland, of a Chinese father and a Maori mother. He had outraged his middle class parents by consorting with inner city Maori gangs and festooning his face and body with garish tribal tattoos. A football scholarship had taken him to Hawaiian Pacific University, where he had picked up the game of tennis. Despite his lack of experience, he had the classic strokes and footwork of a club pro. His serve was a blur, his forehand a topspin horror that would bite hard on the asphalt before leaping at your face.

But Joe and I had a chance against this formidable duo, because as a doubles team we were not exactly chopped liver. I have played serious tennis since high school, and Joe, albeit a dabbler, is a former college basketball player with fine athletic skills. He's also a competitor. The first time we played each other I was whipping him pretty good and he was clearly not enjoying the experience. Late in the second set, when he was at the baseline struggling with my powerful, deep drives, I tormented him with a sudden drop shot that he could not possibly reach in time. As a show of disdain, I turned my back to the net and started to walk to the service line even as the ball was taking its first bounce and Joe was lurching forward in aspects of rage and futility. Two seconds later I was astonished as the ball whizzed past my ear and landed a few inches inside the baseline. When I turned around Joe was at the net, smiling arrogantly. We argued a bit, but there were no spectators present who might have supported my claim that Joe had obviously picked up the ball on its second bounce and hurled it over the net.

So I expected Joe to fight hard against our foes, and he did not disappoint me. For ninety minutes we clawed and scrambled our way into a third set tiebreaker. The score stood thus: 4-6, 7-5, 6-6. And we were up in the tiebreaker, 9-8. It was my serve. I had the match on my racket, as they say. I was serving to Kanogo and that was good, because his strength was not the return of serve. His chops at my blazing cannonball tended to come back as wounded ducks that Joe would crush into oblivion. I stood at the baseline, facing Kanogo in the ad court, breathing steadily, reminding myself to bend my knees as I began my toss. But my toss drifted to a spot behind my head, and I was forced to step back and catch it in my hand. One of the basic rules of serving is never to hit a bad toss, but this is also a slight breach of tennis etiquette. That tennis should even *have* etiquette seems antiquated to me. Tennis is a *mano a mano* fight for dominance. In basketball you can be at the free throw line and a hundred drunken yahoos are mooning you from the bleachers, but you're just supposed to get on with your shot. In tennis if you abort your serve you are annoying your opponent and this is considered bad form. Borrowing a line from Patrick Rafter, the well-liked Australian pro, I called out "Sorry, Mate."

No one said anything in return. I could feel the tension in the air, the butterflies flailing at my stomach walls. Here I was, a pro athlete, a veteran of many publicly observed sporting contests, and yet this meaningless tennis match was giving me sweaty palms. But that's how it is with competitive males. Ping-pong, shuffleboard, seeing who can spit highest up on the wall. It doesn't matter what the game is—you want to win so bad that it messes with your endocrine system.

Okay, all I had to do was place a reasonably hard serve to Kanogo's backhand. I could take a little off, and he'd still most likely return it somewhere in Joe's vicinity. I readied myself for another try at the serve. The thing about the toss is that you don't *throw* the ball up in the air; you hang onto it until your hand is at its highest point, then simply let go of the ball and watch it ascend, propelled by the momentum of your arm. What I had done before was let go of it too soon. So I moved my arm slowly, and let go of the ball at exactly the right moment, and drove a crisp, rapid serve into the damn net.

I swore under my breath. Why had I been so stupid? Serving to his backhand had forced me to aim the ball at a part of the net that is slightly higher than it is toward the centerline. I had made a tactical error.

Joe turned briefly from his spot at the net and gave me look of confidence and a tightened fist. Now I knew what I had to do. Take a little off my second serve—not too much, just a little—and make sure it landed in the box.

I tossed the ball beautifully, and it hovered in the blue-gray twilight of the sky, awaiting the standard punishing blow. I brought the racket back and bent my legs, just as I was supposed to do. But when I swung forward I felt a sudden, horrifying hesitancy born of fear, and my arm turned to jelly and the racket came down all wrong and once again the ball fizzled into the net.

With neither a word nor a glance Joe picked up the ball and bounced it back to me. His neutrality was a kindness. He knew that I was in mid-choke, and that only I could stop it. Double-faulting to the weaker of the two opponents was a cardinal sin, a sign of nerves. And now the score was tied, and I had to try to regain our advantage by serving one past Phillip Woo.

But I was already a beaten man. Sometimes you just lose it, and that's what had happened during that double-fault. I had come to a fork in the road—victory one way, defeat the other—and I had stumbled toward defeat.

I got my first serve in and Woo returned it to my backhand. My feet, heavy now as they sensed failure, did not move quickly, and by the time I reached the ball it was already coming out of its bounce, and my poorly conceived undercutting swing drove the ball wide of the doubles line.

Now they were up by one—"Championship Point!" Kanogo gleefully hollered—and it was Woo serving to Joe. The ball came like a meteor and Joe caught it by the tip of the racket and it flew off into the chain link fence.

Sniveling coward that I am, I felt glad that Joe had made the final error. But there was no denying who had been the real goat. Joe, friend that he is, chose to focus on the fact that we had almost beaten a pair of younger, stronger opponents, and that I had played quite well throughout. "Yeah," I said, bitterness dripping from my voice, "right up to the moment I double-faulted the match away."

Joe laughed. "You choked. It wasn't the first time, it won't be the last. We all do it."

After enjoying an ostentatious high-five, our opponents were gracious in victory. We shook hands and enjoyed our walk back to the dorms, chattering about the various fine shots we had all made. The cool air of early evening dried the sweat from my arms, and the first stars were coming out, and who cared about one lousy tennis match anyway.

Joe slept in the spare cot in my room. We reminisced long past midnight, and it felt like old times. In the morning, after breakfast, we walked in a fine misting rain to his car.

"Be a good boy," I said, as he was backing out of the parking space.

He leaned his long head out the window. "In life," he said, "you're not a choker."

I hoped he was right.

One breezy afternoon I drove through a park in which a Pop Warner football team was having a practice. I pulled over to observe, fascinated by the sight of tiny children in red and white uniforms running around on the soggy field. They looked top-heavy in their oversized white helmets, milling about in the huddle like aliens gathered around a para-lyzed abductee.

What fun it must be, I thought, to play with uniforms and referees and a cheering crowd at so tender an age. I had missed out on all that. I don't recall hearing anything about Pop Warner when I was a kid, and even if there had been some kind of announcement at school, my parents were too disorganized to have taken any notice. So I played pick-up games in fields that had no yard markers. Rough tackle games that the bigger kids sometimes showed up for. Twenty-two players we could never have gathered; usually it was five or six to a side. We played on crisp windy autumn days and also in gray rain and horizontal driving snow. We tore open our pants at the knees and scraped our elbows bloody.

Sometimes when we were too lazy to go to the park and organize a game, we'd play three-on-three touch football in the street. It didn't matter that there were cars parked by the curbs, or that we had to stop every now and then for traffic. You would actually run pass routes using parked cars as a pick for the guy defending you; you'd run right at him and then break for the narrow space between two cars, and the quarterback would have to hit you at the curb, lofting the pass over the roof of the car. On occasion the pass would be low, and the ball would thump hard on the windshield or land with a loud bang on the hood and we'd look nervously around to see if the car'sowner was coming out his front door to give us hell. One of our neighbors, a Mr. Vavra, had a mint green Olds Cutlass that he doted on, and it drove him crazy that we played near his driveway. His car wasn't even on the street, but sometimes an errant pass or punt would come too close for comfort and he'd scream bloody murder. Tommy Puglisi, who lived on our block and had no fear of adults, used to give him lip, asking why didn't he keep his precious goddamn car in the garage.

There was always trouble with Mr. Vavra. One time he swiped our ball and wouldn't give it back. It was a Saturday afternoon and Tommy ran to get his father. Mr. Puglisi had a couple of Balantines in him, and he swaggered up to Vavra's door in his guinea T-shirt, a fearsome sight with his brown bald head and wide hairy shoulders. Naturally we hoped for a fight, but after a few tense words the two men reached a compromise. The ball was returned, and Mr. Puglisi growled at us that the game was over. Of course we were back out there in a couple of days.

But the best moment of all came when Kevin, probably only ten or eleven at the time, convinced me to let him punt, and he shanked it far to the right and it took one bounce on Vavra's driveway before finding its way through the Cutlass's one open window. Kevin had put all his might into the kick and I guess the ball had some real energy to it, because once it sailed through that one window it knocked around like a bee in a hot bottle, bouncing off the steering wheel and the head rests and the closed windows. We laughed loudly while Kevin hustled up to the car and opened the door and snatched the ball away just as Vavra appeared on his front porch in full roar, and we beat it out of there like thieves running from a bank job.

I was remembering all this while watching the kids in their Pop Warner uniforms, and it disturbed me. In pickup games I had played every position there was: quarterback, end, linebacker, safety, you name it. But these kids would be locked into one position, and that would be it. Worse yet, the coach was a squat, beer-bellied type who never stopped yelling. I couldn't hear what he was saying and maybe it was mostly encouragement, but it still bothered me.

But it was none of my business. I mean, it wasn't like the kids were out there getting *sodomized*. I needed to chill.

I know one thing, though. If I ever have a kid, I'll steer him away from Pop Warner or Pee-wee football or whatever the fuck they call it these days, and send him to the park so he can play pick-up like his daddy did. He can wear a jockstrap and a helmet when he gets to high school.

"In my country," said Klaus Kohler, "the women do as they're told." Klaus was behind the wheel of his forest-green Mercedes Benz. The car had half a million miles on it, but it ran great and he was pleased to have bought it from the retired college professor and his wife who were moving to Arizona. I was in the passenger seat and Ipana Brown was in the rear, paging through a pornographic magazine that featured nude women of color.

"This bitch doin' what she's told because they payin' her," said Brown, holding up the magazine so we could have a look-see at the young African-American fellatrice going to

180

town on a very large penis. I looked away in disgust, since my porno preferences run to lesbian hi-jinx. When I'm becoming aroused by a shot of a naked lady, I don't want some guy's dick in the picture. But just for the record, I'm not real big on porno of any kind. If I can't have a live girl in my arms, I'd rather not think about sex at all.

Klaus, however, studied the photo a good long time. He was able to do this because the car was moving by itself, creeping forward on the tracks of the carwash we were stuck in the middle of. A carwash is a place I almost never patronize, feeling as I do that rainstorms are sufficient to wash the crud off my car. But I'll always tag along when someone else wants to waste his dough in such a fashion. I love the cozy feeling of being implausibly dry and safe under torrents of man-made rain while black hanging strips of rubber batter the windows like the tentacles of a kraken.

Klaus grunted—approval, I guess—then turned to the front. I decided to address his previous comment. "Is that true, Klaus? I thought Germany was a modern country.

Aren't there plenty of kraut feminists, just like we got here?"

"To begin my reply," said Klaus, "I first say that I reject your use of the word 'kraut.' But since your meaning is jocund, I take no violent action. Second, it is true that German women take subordinate role to men, despite having political awareness of feminist principles in some cases."

I thought about this. The black tentacles descended, filling the car with a deafening clatter. In a few seconds we passed beyond their reach. "But why, Klaus? If a woman knows she's a man's equal, why knuckle under to some big dumb brute such as yourself?" I was taking liberties, I knew. But Klaus liked me, probably because I read books and sometimes even talked about them. Klaus had a degree in history from a German university I'd never heard of but which was probably more rigorous than the diploma mills we have over here. Scary appearance and guttural voice aside, he was a smart cookie.

"Again, ignoring your insult, I will reply. German women know that the connection between sexes is theater. They have a role to play, and will get what they want by playing that role. This is good for German men, but we have to be careful. When you rough-house with a dog, you must let the dog win sometimes or he will take a real bite out of you."

"Goddamn right," said Brown. "A woman can fuck you up with her mind worse that a bad-ass motherfucker with a lead pipe."

The Mercedes rolled off the tracks onto the pavement. Klaus carefully wheeled the gleaming car into traffic. "Put another way," I said, "as Sam Johnson wrote, the law has given women so little power because nature has given them so much."

Ipana laughed out loud. "That's true, man."

Sam Johnson, I believe, should be known to all football players, because he and John Madden are dead ringers for each other. I bet they would have gotten on well together, too.

Speaking of dead ringers, The Manchester Purple Demons had a middle linebacker that everyone feared and he looked exactly like Larry Fine, so naturally his nickname was "Stooge." He was Bill Flynn, and he hated the nickname. The unasked question was if he hated it so much, why did he allow his hair to grow out like it did on either side of his bald head? The question remained unasked because no one, not even his teammates, dared ask it. Bill Flynn was so mean and crazy that he was virtually friendless. On the field of play he was an animal. If you were unlucky enough to be on the bottom of a pile with him next to you, he might claw and scratch at your eyes just for the hell of it. His idea of fun was to go to a local park and wangle his way into a pick-up touch football game. He would play nicely for a while, then cunningly deliver a clean but devastating block on some hapless insurance salesman who had no idea what kind of beast he had encountered. The poor man would be on the ground vomiting, or howling and clutching his busted-up knee that would never be the same, and Bill Flynn, who liked causing pain, would feel happy.

During a team meeting Hollis Daft said, "Whatever you do, don't antagonize this guy. Block him hard but then help him up. And it wouldn't hurt to call him Mr. Flynn."

"Shit," said Placebo Washington. "Ain't nobody *that* bad."

But we all wondered.

I had good practices that week. I felt strong and quick, and even a little bit fast, which was unusual for me. Not that I was outrunning anybody, but I was separating good. This entailed running stride for stride with the cover man and lulling him into over-confidence, and all of a sudden moving away at a sharp angle. A separating move created a gap of three or four yards, which was usually all you needed to catch a well-thrown ball.

I knew that my lack of speed had made me a target for derision wherever I played. In sprints I was always the last skill guy to cross the line, and sometimes even a big hulking linebacker would beat me. That happened a few times when I had a tryout with the Giants. But it hadn't mattered too much, because I was so pumped to be in their camp that I executed like a man possessed. Bill Parcells was their coach at the time. Once after I performed disgracefully in a sprint, Parcells singled me out.

"Conners," he said. (He called most of the players by their last names, even if, as in my case, the first name was so unusual or pleasant that most people enjoyed saying it.)

I stood there, breathing hard, waiting.

"Where I live," said Parcells, "there's this old guy sells newspapers. Must be sixty-five, seventy years old. He's a big fat guy, and he limps from having one leg shorter than the other. You know what?"

"What?"

"I'm gonna bring him in here so you can see what it feels like to beat somebody down the field."

Everyone laughed. But after that there was a subtle change in the way I was regarded on and off the field. It was known that the Man wouldn't bust your balls unless he liked you. If you were noticed at all, even to be made fun of, then maybe you had a chance of making the team. It was a shame that I never found out if my shot with the Giants could have been the real deal. A few days later I twisted my ankle making a cut. It swelled up enough to keep me off the field for a week. When I returned, the ankle wasn't at full strength. I fell behind, other guys stepped up, and that was the end of that.

But at least I could say I once played for "The Tuna," even if only in a few scrimmages. They called Parcells "The Tuna" because once

186

when some guys were trying to get over on him about something, he said, "What am I, Charley the Tuna?" He was referring to the character—a talking tuna fish—in an old commercial who never knew what the hell was going on, never saw death at the other end of the hook. But at the time I didn't know this. I thought they called him that because when he would stand on the sidelines with his arms on either side of his ample belly, he looked like a tuna hanging at the end of a dock. I was glad I never told this to anyone at the Giants camp, for they certainly would have delighted in making sure Parcells heard it. Like all good coaches and teachers, Parcells had the power to make men strive. I hadn't stuck with the Giants, but in the back of my mind now was the thought that if I had even one good year with the Cossacks, I might run into Parcells someday and find out that he'd heard about it. I wanted to shake The Tuna's hand at a sports banquet and hear him say, "You did a nice job with Centerport, Fin." I believe Parcells would use my first name at such a moment.

The Purple Demons brought a cold autumn rain into our house on Wednesday night. And they came to play. A good runback of the opening kickoff had them on the 47. Three plays later Alton Wingate, their speedy flanker, was dancing in the end zone after hauling in a 30-yard strike from quarterback Greg Lawson.

Walt Watson could only manage to bring the ensuing kickoff to the 19. The offense stunk it up, and we were three-and-out. Austin Goudy boomed a punt to the Manchester 35, but the return man, a wisp of smoke named Willis Croix, darted through the coverage for forty yards before Goudy made a touchdown-saving, shoe-string tackle near the sideline. The defense held, and Manchester settled for a field goal.

We couldn't get anything going, and the score remained 10-0 into the fourth quarter. Part of the problem was that safety Carthage Lee had decided to give some shit to Stooge Flynn. Lee was a tough kid on a football high, and when he ran to the sideline with the rest of the defense and caught sight of Flynn trotting onto the field with his helmet off, he couldn't help himself.

"Yo, Stooge!" he yelled. "Over here, Stooge! I'm *talkin'* to you, ugly motherfucker!"

Flynn had been lifting his helmet to pull it on, but when he heard Lee he kept it off for a moment, as if in defiance. It was apparent he'd been working on a mustache, but it didn't help any. In fact, it made him look funnier. Carthage Lee had a comment about that, too. "You can grow all the hair you want on that ugly-ass face, it ain't gonna make no difference. You still be lookin' like Larry the motherfuckin' stooge."

This happened right after halftime. For all of the third quarter Stooge Flynn was a nightmare to behold, keening and slavering as he pulled ball carriers down so hard their heads bounced on the turf, stabbing through face guards at the soft flesh of blockers' cheeks with his gnarled, awful fingers. By the start of the fourth quarter, we made sure Carthage Lee was keeping his big mouth shut.

With seven minutes to play, we finally got it together. Judson Trask ripped off some nice chunks of yardage, and I contributed a diving catch over the middle for 18 yards.

Now the ball was on the Manchester 15. It was third down, and the play called for me to line up as a second tight end, slip through the middle, outrun the coverage, and catch

189

the ball for a touchdown. That would put us within three points, and we could try an onside kick.

At the snap I chip-blocked the outside linebacker and cut toward the center of the field. Stooge Flynn was fooled by Danielson's play-action fake to Charley Hooks, and dove toward the middle. The wideouts ran short fly patterns to the corners of the end zone, so the way was clear. I raced untouched over the goal line and looked up for the pass. But the big Manchester defensive line was pushing the guards and tackles back, collapsing the pocket. Even at 6'2", Danielson was dwarfed by the surge of Purple Demons with their arms up and waving.

Then from out of the chaos it came, a tight spiral barely brushing the straining fingers of a defensive tackle. Alas, that brush altered the ball's trajectory just enough to turn an easy pass into a tough catch. I had half a second to take one long stride and leap high for the ball. For a moment I felt it in my hands, and then it was gone, vanished like a melon in a magic trick. Simultaneously I was hit by the free safety, a slab of concrete moving at hyperspeed. I landed on my back, somehow still conscious, aware of total body pain not diminished at all by the lovely panorama of flashing stars and ringed planetoids that danced in my vision. Somebody helped me to my feet and I hobbled to the sideline.

Reg Hastings kicked the easy field goal, making it 10-3. We tried the onside kick and failed to recover the ball, so I was off the hook for my drop. Without the ball we couldn't have scored again anyway.

It was a quiet locker room. Many of the players had made mental mistakes and physical errors. Lou gathered the team around him in the center of the room. He reminded everyone that we had a winning record and there was still half a season to play. This was a wakeup call. "Remember," he said, "every failure carries within it the seeds of future victories."

Some minutes later, while dressing after his shower, Kenny Liebowitz called out to Lou, who was talking to the trainer. "Coach, I understand what you mean. It's like this game was a rotting pumpkin, all slimy and caving in. And the seeds that fall out of its decaying corpse will make new pumpkins."

"You got it," said Lou, and turned back to the trainer.

Ken mused for a while, tucking his shirt into his pants. "But wait," he said. "Then those pumpkins get all slimy and rotten, too. And the next batch after that. So every failure leads to more failure, after an all too brief moment of victory."

Coy Jessup walked by and threw a sopping jock strap into Ken's face. "No deep philosophizing in the locker room."

There were cheers all around.

On a Sunday afternoon I drove to Laura's house to meet Cody. They lived outside of town a little ways in a bungalow set well back from the road. The front yard was big, the back one even bigger, and there were a few large trees on the property. The plan was for lunch at the house and a drive to an ice cream parlor for dessert. I had suggested a movie, but Cody had already seen everything any good that was playing in town.

Cody was a handsome boy with light brown hair, small for his age with skinny arms and legs. He shook hands with me on the front porch and right away asked me if I liked to play Frisbee. As it happens, I am a Frisbee player of long standing and considerable skill, so we walked to the back yard for a little sport while Laura prepared lunch.

The day was overcast and blustery. Gusts of wind lifted the apple-green Frisbee high into the air, where it would hover and bob. Cody was good at both running and catching. He knew how to judge the angle at which the Frisbee would sink, and would run to the spot where it was headed. I praised the boy, knowing he was trying to show off something he could do well. But it was not false praise; Cody was a very decent Frisbee player.

Over a lunch of roast chicken with stuffing, green beans and mashed potatoes, Cody talked animatedly about school, his friends, movies he liked, his favorite video games. He asked me some questions about playing football and listened carefully to the answers. That's one of the great things about kids. They don't just nod and think about what they want to say next while you're telling them something. Unless, I suppose, you're a parent telling them how to behave.

It turned out that Laura and Cody hadn't made it to the Manchester game. Cody had run a fever, and she thought it unwise to take him out in the chilly night. That was okay with me, considering my fourth quarter muff of a possible touchdown pass. But then she told me she'd seen the play on ESPN's SportsCenter, which she watched that night for the express purpose of learning the outcome of the game. Unfortunately, my botched play had been shown numerous times as the "hit of the day."

Let me tell you, I'm not so crazy about ESPN. I am of the opinion that they tend to focus on the negative. But I guess that makes me a hypocrite, because I always watch with unconcealed delight when the network shows some jack-in-the-box losing it at the podium and offering to fistfight a reporter for asking a stupid question.

After lunch we drove to Ben & Jerry's for ice cream cones. We took our treats out to the car, which I had cleaned and aired out so it wouldn't smell like sweaty clothes and old newspapers. We parked by the lake and sat there talking, eating, watching dark clouds coast across the autumn sky. A drop of ice cream fell from my cone and onto my pants. Right away Laura took a napkin and dipped it into the plastic cup of water they'd given her at Ben & Jerry's. Gently, without a word, she rubbed the ice cream off my pants, just above the knee. She looked up and smiled at me for a second, then held the crumpled napkin in front of her face. "Trash?"

"I usually just toss it in the back," I said. "But I'm changing my ways." I took a plastic bag out of the glove compartment and handed it to her. I said nothing about the wifely chore she had unexpectedly performed, and neither did she.

I didn't want the outing to end, but I had a team meeting at six. I took them home and Cody rushed right in to catch some TV show that was just starting. On the front porch I asked Laura if she'd like to go out with me again, and she said she would. Then she leaned forward slightly, a little nervous, but intent on being properly kissed. I placed my hands on her shoulders and bent my head slightly and obliged her. It was a gentle, lingering kiss. Our lips parted slowly, with mutual smiles.

As I drove to the meeting I knew that thoughts of my new girlfriend would sustain me as I endured the droning voices of assistant coaches amid the shiftings of large, bored men in uncomfortable chairs.

We sat on Laura's porch in hazy twilight. Cody and his friend Johanna were chasing Marbles, the cat, back and forth across the expansive lawn. The kids were shrieking with laughter, and Marbles was having a fine old time as well. The cat was in control, Laura said, and when he tired of the game would simply disappear into the weeds.

For no reason, I suppose, other than she thought it was time, Laura decided to talk about her ex-husband. So far I had been re-spectfully indifferent to the details of her failed marriage, limiting myself to wondering if the ex was still in the picture in any way. She had said no, that he was a shit who had turned his back on them. I knew there were always two sides to a story, but I didn't press. Now she told me the rest of it.

It wasn't much, really.

After college and a couple of boyfriends, she had married an ex-serviceman who made his living as a carpenter. She'd been a wait-ress at a restaurant where Dan and his co-workers would take lunch while on some con-

struction job, and she liked his aggressive-
ness—he kept asking her out even though
she made it clear that he was not her type.
He was a roughneck, not good-looking or par-
ticularly well spoken, but he kept trying, and
finally she gave in. He seemed nice, and he
was big and manly, and he rode a Harley. He
told her he wasn't just some bruiser (he had
boxed professionally, or so he said—she
never saw any clippings) but had plans to
better himself. He hoped to get a degree and
go into business. He wanted a house with a
fireplace and a yard full of little kids running
around. He treated her like a queen, she said,
and the chemistry wasn't bad. (This meant
the sex had been good, but she didn't want to
say that, exactly, for which I was grateful.)

At the wedding there was drunkenness
and lewd advances made upon the bride and
her bridesmaids and three fistfights, all of
this engendered by Dan's family. In less than
a month of marriage to Laura, Dan lost his
job, got busted for DUI, and gave her a fat lip.
He stopped drinking for a while and things
got better. But then a famous friend of his,
an old army buddy named Grabowski, came
to visit from California, and the drinking

started again. Dan said that his friend had a genius mind that had not been tamed by formal education. Laura just saw a bum who camped out on their sofa pounding down beers and making weighty pronouncements about the stuff he saw on TV. A year of Dan and his ways was all she could take, but even as she was filing for divorce she learned that she was pregnant. In desperation they'd had one boozy frolicsome night and she had neglected her contraception, and the result would be Cody. She thought briefly of abortion, but could not bear to end the life of the small creature inside her that was growing larger each day with blind unthinking hope.

Laura took a sip of tea from the steaming mug in her hands and drew her feet up under the blanket covering her lap. Slowly she rocked back and forth in the old maple rocking chair she'd had since her girlhood. Her tale was ordinary. Not even backup material for the Jerry Springer show. But it was sordid nonetheless. I could tell she was embarrassed to tell it. She was soft-spoken and well-read, worked in a library, dressed nice and didn't use profanity. I couldn't imagine her liquored up and shouting, her legs wrapped around a poorly-shaven, foul-breathed biker. But women are full of surprises.

"Well," I said, "we all make mistakes."

The twilight had deepened. The shouts and laughter of the boy and girl playing on the lawn remained vibrant, but their shapes had become ghostlike. A bit uneasily, Laura called out to them.

"Cody, Johanna! Better come in now. It's getting late."

Without protest the children ran toward the porch. After they clumped up the stairs, I said "Hey, who's up for McDonald's? My treat."

Two piercing voices sang out "Me!" in unison. Laura gave me a wry smile. A little Mickey D's never hurt anybody. And she wouldn't have to cook. "Call your parents," she said to Johanna. "See if it's okay."

I drove the three miles to the nearest Golden Arches. The kids bubbled in the back seat. Laura sat next to me, lost in thought. It was chilly, so I had the heater on. I pulled into the drive-through and ordered my usual: three burgers, ketchup and onions only, and a coke. No fries. In the old days the fries were cooked in animal fat and were damn tasty.

Now all the aging yuppies are worried about their cholesterol so no more animal fat. And the fries are lousy. Laura wanted a grilled chicken sandwich and a coke. For Cody and Johanna, cheeseburgers devoid of pickles and onions (lest they gag), plenty of fries, and an Oreo McFlurry each.

When I pulled up to the pay window, I felt the urge to crack wise at the pimply kid handing us our bags, but I didn't. I have an unfortunate tendency to engage service people in banter. Usually it's fine, because my manner is agreeable and they take me for a harmless fool. I get it honest, as they say, because Dad did this all the time. Here's a story to show you what I mean. Dad and a co-worker enter a furniture store. They've just received their Christmas bonuses, and the co-worker wants to blow his on a reclining chair. Dad is along for the ride. He sits at a dining room table and takes his pay envelope out of his pocket, starts counting his money. An eager salesman appears, rubbing his hands together. May I help you, sir? he asks. No thanks, says Dad, I can count it myself.

I carry on the tradition without even thinking about it. The haircut I'd gotten the other day was at a beauty school—trainees operating at a scary-low price. A sign out front read, *All Male Haircuts--$5.* I walked in and said to the girl at the desk, "I'm all male, so let's get started."

But my brother Kevin is the champ. He denies it, but I'm certain that he thinks up fancy comebacks in advance. I read somewhere that Oscar Wilde used to do this. Another Irishman.

One sweltering day Kevin and I walked into a hardware store and the clerk said to us, "Hot enough for you?"

"You bet," said Kevin. "It's hotter out there than a freshly fisted fag in a fuchsia frock."

The clerk, a stocky man in a short-sleeved white shirt that contrasted nicely with his large, tanned forearms, looked hard at us for a moment, but let it drop. Out on the sidewalk I said, "One of these days you're going to say the wrong thing to the wrong guy."

"Nah," said Kevin. "All the world loves a quipster."

We ate our take-out dinner in the parking lot, then took Johanna home. I was all set to drop Laura and Cody off, but Laura invited me in. We watched some TV while Cody slurped down the rest of his McFlurry. Laura said, "I have to get Cody ready for bed. Will you wait here till we're done?"

"Sure," I said. Laura got up off the couch and on the way out she gave my shoulder an affectionate squeeze.

I looked at the TV but didn't notice what was on. I turned it off. Looks like this is the night, I thought.

The wind had picked up. Huge gusts shook the walls of the small house. I heard the rapid thudding of Cody's feet as he ran up and down the hallway. I felt enrobed by the warmth and coziness of a home. From the kitchen came the rasp of the fridge blowing its freezing breath on trays of ice. The furnace clicked on. Hot air rose from metal registers on the hardwood floors. The timbers of the house creaked and groaned as they expanded from within. Muffled sounds came through the ceiling. A faucet opening, then closing. A dialogue between mother and son, good-naturedly combative. The faucet opening and closing again, followed by a shuddering protest from the piping that snaked its way through the walls down to the cellar. The gasp and release of the toilet.

Then Cody was at the top of the stairs. "Goodnight, Fin!" he shouted.

I stood up and turned to face the stairway. "Goodnight, Cody. Have good dreams."

"I will!" Cody ran down the hall to his bedroom, and in a moment I heard the violent *thunk* a bed makes when a seventy-pound projectile lands upon it.

"Hey!" shouted Laura. Then all was quiet.

I knew the boy was excited to have me around. It gave me a pang, thinking about this. I remembered those rare nights when both my parents had been home, and I had felt warm and happy under the covers, vibrating with joy as I heard them talking and laughing downstairs.

What would it be like, I wondered, to have Laura and the boy with me all the time? Now I was visualizing the three of us on the way to Disney World, a happy family laughing it up in a minivan. A bit premature, considering that Laura and I hadn't even been naked together.

That consideration put my mind where it needed to be.

I went into the kitchen and cupped a handful of water and swished it around in my mouth, washing away the lingering burger and onion foulness. If there'd been some liquor in the house I would have poured myself a shot. But Laura didn't even drink beer. She didn't care for the taste. I knew there was a bottle of wine in the cabinet, but it was unopened and I didn't need a drink that badly. Hell, I didn't need a drink at all; I was just feeling a little tense.

I heard the creak of floorboards and turned around. Laura stood in the doorway of the kitchen. She'd crept up on me in soft down slippers. Except for the footwear, she hadn't slipped into something more comfortable. (What was I expecting, a French Maid's uniform? In *this* drafty house?) In fact, she'd put on a bulky red wool sweater. But it didn't matter; she looked wonderful, her lips moist, her eyes shining, her blonde hair framing her flushed face. She held her arms folded across her chest. "Shall we see what's on TV?"

I wiped my wet hands on a towel that hung from a hook next to the sink. Through the kitchen window I saw the lights of a neighbor's house winking on and off as the leafy limbs of a large old maple tree swayed back and forth in the tumultuous wind. I turned from the sink and she unfolded her arms and reached out to me. We kissed and the tension in our bodies melted like snow on a radiator.

I picked her up—she felt light as a girl—and made like Errol Flynn, carrying her into the living room. This act of gallantry was no big deal for a professional athlete, but the nearby couch, not the stairway and the bedroom beyond, seemed a good enough destination for now. So I knelt down next to the couch and eased her onto it. Still kneeling, I bent forward to kiss her again, and set my hands to wandering beneath her sweater, thrilled by the contact of my palms with the soft skin of her bare midriff. I moved up to her bra and she didn't stop me. But I was still kneeling, bending over her. I felt awkward, like a dwarf pawing a courtesan stretched out on a settee. Laura rescued the moment by rolling off the couch and collapsing on top of me. For the next few minutes we made out on the floor like a couple of teens in a rumpus room. I would have been happy to take her right there on the rug, but she stopped me and said we should go to the bedroom.

We walked up the stairs hand in hand. We ducked into Cody's room and satisfied ourselves that he was deep in a child's traveling sleep. In her bedroom Laura pulled down the blankets and sheet and sat on the edge of the mattress. She let me undress her, and my gratitude was inexpressible. Her wool sweater, her T-shirt, her bra, her slacks, her panties—I removed each garment with the tenderness of a priest handling sacred vestments, because each revelation of her flesh reminded me that undressing a woman for the first time is a proper moment for religious feelings.

My own clothes came off without reverence and I scootched under the covers. We did not hurry, and it was sweet and satisfying, quite lovely for a first time

We lay fused, spent, softly murmuring to each other. In our exertions we had kicked off the covers, and now became aware of the sweat evaporating off our skins in the cool air of the bedroom. I reached for the comforter and pulled it up over us. In the cozy warmth we talked as lovers will, and grew sleepy, and eventually I drifted into a happy, dreamless sleep.

The Cossacks bordered a chartered bus at ten a.m. and settled in for the long ride through Pennsylvania. It was a pleasantly late start, and we were a well-rested, well-fed bunch. The bus was headed for Altoona, where we would meet the Gorgons.

Except for the Rutland Moose, teams in the Northeastern Football Association had very cool names. Already we'd played against Dervishes, Berserkers, and Purple Demons. Now it was Gorgons. Naturally their logo was the head of Medusa with her 'do of fanged serpents. It was a logo the sportswriters were having fun with. When Mack Tremaine, Altoona's heavy-legged fullback, had a game in which he was tackled many times behind the line of scrimmage, a scribe speculated that perhaps he had stared too long at the team logo and was turning into a monolith.

The betting line had us up by ten points, because Altoona wasn't any good. They were winless, and the locals were taking it hard, since so many tough, successful players had come out of the area. Johnny Unitas, Joe

Montana, Joe Namath, Mike Ditka, Jack Ham, Jim Kelly and Tony Dorsett were all products of Western Pennsylvania. But the Gorgons had no roster of all-stars. Injuries and bad personnel decisions had saddled them with a forty-year-old quarterback with a drinking problem, a middle linebacker who beat up his girlfriends but couldn't tackle opposing runners, and a tight end who was the paradigm of unfulfilled promise.

The tight end was Scotty Kay, and in his youth he had been a golden-haired wonder from the plains of Kansas. A 220-pound fireball who broke every rushing record in the state, he was given a full ride to Notre Dame. He chose football even though he could hit a baseball a country mile and averaged thirty points per game as a power forward. He ran so fast there was talk he might go to the Olympics, and the first time he ever picked up a racket he whipped the number one guy on his high school tennis team. In his sophomore year with the Irish, he made All-American. He had a dazzling smile and a way with words that agents knew would allow him to write his own ticket when it came to endorsements and a post-football career in broadcasting. But having been raised properly, he kept the agents at bay while he was at Notre Dame; he wasn't the type to lose his college eligibility by accepting a free weekend at some huckster's suite in the Trump Towers. Coeds swooned at his feet, but he was the kind of boy who went steady with one girl at a time, and he chose Lornabelle Slye, a treacle-sweet Georgia gal studying Theater Arts, a very focused young lady who had her eye on the Miss America Pageant. The kid had it all. His life was playing out like every man's dream.

But there was just one problem. Scotty Kay was a coprophile.

By his senior year there were signs of trouble. On the field he ran with less fire and abandon, and he was starting to make mental errors. Off the field he seemed distant, distracted. Rumors of drugs and gambling evaporated when there was simply no evidence to support them. Nor was there any trouble back home in Kansas—his family was fine. Two siblings still in school and a Norman Rockwell mom and pop who worked the farm and seldom stayed up past ten. Lornabelle appeared happy as could be, mincing in high heels at her swain's side and beaming at photographers, or gracing a proffered microphone with her customary "How y'all doin' tonight?"

NFL scouts were worried, but they looked at his combine stats, at his powerful, chiseled frame, and made him the first pick in the draft. He went to the Cleveland Browns, down and out at the bottom of the league. The Browns needed a savior, and in training camp Scotty Kaye exceeded their expectations. In the first exhibition game, against Dallas but played in Mexico City, of all places, and globally televised, the whole world watched him rack up 140 yards and three touchdowns in the first half alone, and afterward the Cleveland media proclaimed him "the white Jim Brown."

Then came the first bombshell. Lornabelle held a press conference to announce that the engagement was off. Affecting the devastated look of a teary Marilyn Monroe on the day she dumped the Yankee Clipper, sweet Lornabelle spoke of "profound differences" and hinted at a dark secret that she would take to her grave. Then she rested her head on her lawyer's shoulder and was bundled back into her apartment.

One week later, having decided that there was too much time between now and the grave, she made a pre-publicized appearance on a shock-jock's radio show to spill the beans. And these were some beans.

Millions of the shock-jock's fans listened to Lornabelle's sobs and sighs as she struggled to tell her story, to reveal the terrible secret that had destroyed her hopes and dreams. The shock-jock's rich, sonorous voice oozed sensitivity and compassion as he gently coaxed her along. Finally she blurted it out, the famous line that all who heard will never forget: *"He only wanted me for my BMs."*

It was a stunner. There were loud groans and outcries from the shock-jock's sidekicks. But the shock-jock, ever composed, still in sensitive voice, seized the moment to ask the penetrating question, "Let us be clear on this. By BMs, do you mean bowel movements?"

Though heaving with sobs, the shattered girl managed to explain that yes, it was true, and although she'd begged Scotty to get help, he'd refused, and she could no longer live a lie. Not surprisingly, the switchboard began to light up. A few nasty callers suggested that Lornabelle had opted to come forth only when her bid for a shot at Miss America had fallen short. Others—women, mostly—had definite ideas of what should be done to Scotty Kay. The shock-jock was full of questions. He wanted details. But Lornabelle was finished— for now. She was writing a book that would tell the whole tragic story, and she was also soon to be featured in a Penthouse pictorial, and oh, by the way, she had a website.

And just like that, Scotty Kay's dream was over. He checked into a psychiatric clinic and stayed there a long time. He gave back his bonus money. When he got out of the clinic he went home to Kansas. There his parents sheltered him, quietly turning away the media vultures who kept coming to the farm. In time the controversy wore itself out. And then a remarkable thing happened. Everyone became respectful of his sorrow. There were no more interviews with Lornabelle, no more tabloid ink given to hookers claiming to have been part of Scotty Kay's stool seraglio.

A year later the Oakland Raiders came calling. The Raiders' logo was a pirate with an eye-patch and a dagger in his mouth. The team had always been a last-stop for misfits and thugs. It was a hook-up that made sense.

In camp Scotty ran well. He was fit and full of desire, and they gave him a shot at the starting job. But there were problems. He'd taken a liking to drink, to its anesthetic properties. At night, after a day of feeling the smirks and stares of curious fans, he would dull his brain with whiskey. It took a toll. Mornings he was shaky. In scrimmages he missed blocking assignments, forgot his pass routes. And in the stands there was always some clown ready to give him a resounding raspberry, a noise usually delivered as a fartful commentary on ineptitude, but now freighted with associations of so much more than mere flatulence. No one on the field ever did that, and it said a lot for Scotty that his peers refused to take advantage of his vulnerability. No matter how badly they wanted to win, they would not kick this tortured man who had fallen so low. But among the fans? Forget it. Scotty could be sure to hear some big fat loser working on his ninth beer who thought it hilarious to razz the guy with the poop fetish. So it was inevitable that one humid night in Miami, during the final game of the preseason, Scotty Kay climbed into the seats and severely beat one of his tormentors before being subdued by security guards.

One of the great things about this country, I contend, is the feeling always in the air that a guy should get another chance. As long as you're sorry—even better, if you cry on TV like a shamed preacher man— Americans will tell you go ahead, give it another shot. Scotty never went on TV to talk about his problem, but he didn't have to. His haunted face bore the pain of lost promise. You could see it in his eyes.

Now, a few years later, he'd been given a last chance with the Altoona Gorgons. He was twenty pounds heavier and slower of foot, but still probably more gifted than anyone else in the NFA. They'd put him at tight end, and every once in a while he would make a catch and run that took your breath away. I was glad to be an offensive player. When the Gorgons had the ball I could stand on the sidelines and watch Scotty Kay.

The drive to Altoona seemed to take forever. I had a window seat, and Kenny Liebowitz kept leaning across me to point out the carnage of road kill. It was the start of mating season for deer, he explained, so bucks were chasing does all over the place and in their sex frenzy paid less attention to the rules of the road. The evidence was there, whizzing past, horrible to see. There were many fresh kills, deer bodies exploded into gory sections by barreling semis, dark blood staining the asphalt.

"This is why I don't eat meat," said Kenny.

"I don't see the connection," I said. "I feel sorry for the poor things, too. But this is the open road, not a meat-packing plant. My craving for a burger isn't causing this to happen."

"In a way it is, Fin. It's just another link in the chain of man treating animals as material. You know why there's all these deer running around getting splattered by buses and shit? Because we killed off all the predators. The wolves and mountain lions. So there's nothing out there to keep the deer population in check. Except cars. Oh, and hunters. Let's not forget the hunters. Man, you want to talk about bad karma."

"Shut up, Kenny," I said. "You're giving me a headache."

"That's what everyone tells me when they don't want to hear the truth."

I knew that he would keep on talking, like he always did. But it didn't matter because I fell asleep anyway. It was a fitful, sweaty sleep, not at all satisfying, but when I awoke we were in the city of Altoona. Now it was Kenny's job to point out the many street signs named, for some crazy reason, after English poets like Browning, Keats, and Wordsworth. "You see?" said Kenny. "I'd make a great tour guide."

The game was a wipeout.

We pounded the Gorgons 47-14. Placebo Washington added two touchdown passes to his league-leading total, and the defense came up big with five interceptions. The only negative was Judson Trask breaking his ankle on the second play of the game. He was running a sweep around left end when he saw the outside linebacker over-commit. So he stopped short and darted up into the seam, and Paul Facemeyer, his own damn teammate, the tackle who was supposed to

216

be leading the play, got his legs confused and fell over onto Judson, knocking him down and shattering his ankle. Judson lay on his back thrashing his head and slamming the ground with his arms, partly from the pain but also from the frustration of knowing his season was done. Walt Watson came in as a backup, but he had the flu and was ineffective. So Ray Whipple got his first chance to show what he could do.

I could see that Ray had lost a step, but pure speed had never been his strength anyway. He was shifty, a start-and-stop artist who could turn a graceful cornerback into Herman Munster. Ray carried the ball 12 times and gained 90 yards, a hell of a performance. He also caught a couple of passes for short gains, and made a nifty block on a blitzing safety, enabling Mike Ponsonby to throw a 16-yard strike over the middle for my only catch of the day.

It felt right and proper to be in the game at the same time with my pal, just like in the old days. And Ray had needed this very badly. Before we'd climbed on the bus for Altoona, a cheerful elderly man in a brown polyester suit had served Ray with his divorce papers.

Ray was happy enough in the locker room after the game, but by the time we boarded the bus he'd grown quiet. He sat next to me and barely said a peep. So I napped a little, and looked out the window at the dark shapes of the Pennsylvania hills passing in the night, and napped a little more, and idly paged through a worn issue of *People* I'd found under the seat, and finally, out of boredom, tried to draw Ray into conversation. "How about that Scotty Kay?" I said. Scotty Kay had scored the Gorgons' only two touchdowns, both in the first quarter, one on a spectacular broken field run of 60 yards. Then he'd sat out the rest of the game, and no one knew why.

"He's still a player," said Ray.

I prattled on for a while about the game and Scotty Kay and a few other things, then fell silent when Ray failed to respond with more than a grunt or two. I lay back in my seat and closed my eyes, surrendering to the bumpy rhythms of the road and the thrumming engine of the bus.

"I wonder how he did it?" said Ray.

I stayed at rest, eyes closed. "Who? Did what?"

"Scotty Kay. How the hell do you come back from that much public humiliation? How do you do it?"

"I don't know, Ray. I guess he still has it inside. Desire. The will to compete."

I felt Ray move in his seat. He was taking something out of his coat pocket. I heard the crackle of a wrapper and opened my eyes. Ray had a large Nestle Crunch bar in his hand.

I extended my palm. "Don't mind if I do," I said, taking the initiative.

Ray started to unwrap the candy bar. "Wait," I said. "Here. Do it this way." I grabbed it from Ray and broke it in half, still unwrapped.

"What the hell are you doing?"

"I don't want your fingers all over the chocolate," I said. I held the Crunch bar in both hands. It was collapsed in the center, floppy like a broken arm in a sleeve.

"Go ahead, take half," said Ray, scowling.

Daintily, I tore the candy bar in two equal portions. Some of the chocolate flaked off and fell into my lap, but it was a pretty neat job on the whole. I handed Ray his half, then peeled back the wrapper and the inner foil and took a bite, savoring the nubby texture and the sweetness of it.

"You know," said Ray, "I'm gonna be fine. Just fine."

"Damn straight," I said.

"It doesn't make any sense to get all broken-hearted over a cunt who doesn't want me, right?"

"Right."

"Time to get on with my new life."

"Full speed ahead."

"Hell, I'm a good-looking guy. There'll be plenty of babes after me, right?"

I said nothing. I nibbled away at my half of the Crunch bar.

"You're an asshole," said Ray.

I laughed. Then I hit Ray on the arm hard enough so it hurt. "And you're an easy mark. Come on, man, get real. Of *course* you're a good-looking guy. You wanna hear what Bobby Hertzig said about you?"

Ray breathed a heavy sigh. He pushed the rest of the candy into his mouth and wiped his fingers on the cloth armrest. It was three a.m. and the bus was quiet, everyone sleeping or reading. I settled in for some more sleep, too.

"So what kind of stuff did Bobby say about me?" asked Ray.

I started seeing Laura regularly, two, three times a week, and it was good. After a day of meetings and practice I would show up at her door and we would have dinner and put Cody to bed and then tuck ourselves in for a few hours of fun. I usually left by eleven, but one night I fell asleep until two a.m. I woke up knowing I had to put on my clothes and head back to the dorm. It was a cold, quiet night. The candle on Laura's nightstand had gone out, and the room was dark. I find the darkness comforting. I wonder when, exactly, it happened, the shift in consciousness from being terrified of the dark to feeling soothed by its embrace. I certainly remember its terrors. One night in particular I'll never forget. An inattentive baby sitter had allowed Debbie and me to watch *Invasion of the Body Snatchers* on the late show. It was the original black and white version from the fifties, the creepiest movie ever made, I believe. I must have been seven or eight, and I spent the next few nights like a statue with the covers pulled up over my head, not moving a muscle, barely breathing because I knew the pod people were standing next to the bed, waiting to get me.

But now I love the dark, and lying there in the cozy blackness it was hard to disengage from Laura. After the release of sex she had fallen into a deep sleep marked by twitches of her whole body that made me think of heat lightning. Silent flashes in the far distance of her dreams. She came awake and moaned as I gently lifted her leg off mine and kissed her shoulder in compensation for leaving the bed. I said don't get up but she wasn't having it. She put on her robe and walked me downstairs, sleepy-eyed and barefoot. At the door she hugged me tightly, and stepped onto the tops of my shoes. "Floor's cold," she said.

"You forgot your slippers."

She kissed me then, in a melting way that said come back to bed with me now and spend the night and forget everything else. But that wasn't an option. I had practice in the morning. I could do nothing to jeopardize my tenuous connection to the world of professional football. Screwing up now would blow my chances to catch on somewhere as a coach, and then I'd have nothing, not even the girl, because no matter how starry-eyed in love two people might be, once the job and the money go out the window, all the colors fade from the rainbow.

Things were looking good for the Cossacks. We were perched atop our division. Portland was next. Beat them and it was clear sailing to the Championship game, probably against Manchester, who'd already beaten us once but would not do it again if we had anything to say about it.

In meetings we were alert, on the practice field sharp. We had a sense of being a team, of having a shared goal. And in the back of each man's mind simmered personal hopes and ambitions. We worked hard not only for the sake of the team, but for our own individual futures.

A buzz had developed around the NFA. Exciting players had surfaced and the national media were paying attention. Next week an HBO crew was coming in to do a story on Placebo Washington, who was being touted as the next Randy Moss. Everyone was happy for Placebo, but we all hoped to get in on the action.

It was too bad HBO didn't arrive a day earlier, when James Veltry and Bobby Hertzig had a terrific punch-up during practice. They could have filmed the damn thing, and done an up-close-and-personal story on the gay scene in pro football, such as it was.

Actually, the fight took everyone by surprise. The James and Bobby show was supposed to be long gone. Tears had been shed, harsh words exchanged, and both boys had moved on, or so it was thought. On the morning of the fight, at breakfast, Bobby had spoken in loud tones of his new boyfriend, a blond farm boy with a huge pecker. Veltry sat nearby quietly devouring his bacon and eggs. No big deal.

But on the field during passing drills, things got ugly. Whenever Veltry went out, Bobby made sure to cover him, and there was plenty of hard hitting. Veltry, a proud man, started throwing elbows during his routes. I decided to step in, but it was too late. Veltry ran a down-and-in and Bobby shadowed him stride for stride, and I distinctly heard him shout, "You're just a fucking whore!" a moment before he rammed his forearm into Veltry's neck.

Veltry went down. But he was up in a flash and the two ex-lovers tore off their helmets and went at it toe to toe. Players ran over, yelling "Fight! Fight!" When they saw who it was, there were some shouts of "Catfight! Catfight!" After trading a few punches they fell to the turf in a tangle. Lou Levine pushed through the crowd blowing his whistle, and some of the players stepped in at that point and pulled the combatants apart. "Come on, girls," yelled Lou, "you want to settle this, we'll have a bake-off."

Practice resumed. The two boys kept away from each other. What the hell, a little intrasquad fighting was *good* for a football team.

The Portland Narwhales came to town showcasing a halfback named True Lewis that teams were having trouble stopping. Coach Gargano decided the best strategy would be to spy the shifty and powerful Lewis with our toughest, nastiest linebacker, Luther Moffitt. That meant Luther would key on Lewis all the time, running parallel with him across the line of scrimmage during motion, standing opposite him and screaming horrible imprecations as Lewis waited in his three-point stance for the snap of the ball. At 6'1", 235, Luther was about the same size as True Lewis, and while he was a little slower, he was a whole lot meaner.

On the first play from scrimmage, Luther shot through a gap and nailed Lewis for a loss of five yards. He came through so fast and hit him so hard it was like Lewis had been struck down by a sack of rocks hurled from a catapult. Luther Moffitt jumped up and punched the sky, howling, dragon smoke blasting from his open mouth in the cold night air. This memorable scene was captured in slow motion by the NFL Films crew on hand at the behest of HBO, and HBO would show it during their brief segment about the Cossacks on *Inside the NFL*. They caught it from a ground-level camera, pointing upward. Framed against the black of the night sky and the gauzy glare of the stadium lights, this shot of Luther with his bare muscular arms pumping and drops of spit flying out alongside the puffs of vapor caught the essence of football as war. Luther was a gladiator, a barbarian swordsman, a Zulu warrior. A Cossack.

For the first half he was the alpha pit bull of the defense. You could hear his trash-talk from the sidelines: *"I wanna gouge out your eyes and stomp on 'em! I'm gonna hit you so hard you'll wake up in the phantom zone!"*

The Narwhales were stunned, down at the half 28-0. Phillip Woo had three picks, one of which he ran back 45 yards for a touchdown. Ray Whipple squeezed through a pair of buffalo-bodied defensive tackles for a 2-yard score. I got in the game for one play early in the second quarter and made the best of it. Drew Danielson was looking for Placebo Washington downfield, but the coverage was there so he tried to scramble, not something he was very good at. Portland had one outstanding defensive player, Smiley Buchta, a tree-tall, sinewy outside linebacker who was on record saying that aside from killing small game with a pellet gun, nothing ever felt so good to him as seeing the fluttering whites of a quarterback's eyeballs after knocking him senseless. Drew ran for his life, looking for an open man, hearing behind him the rapid, turf-pounding feet of Smiley Buchta closing in like the Grim Reaper on steroids.

I was fifteen yards downfield, suddenly open, waving my arms and yelling like a madman. Drew saw me and hurled a bullet that I snagged while falling to my knees. A safety came up hard but lost his footing and slid past without laying a hand on me. I sprang up and twisted around and saw daylight. It was thirty yards to pay dirt, and the only obstacle in my way was a cornerback coming at me with a good angle.

I have already admitted to a lack of speed, but I am a professional athlete whose body has been trained to respond instinctively under stress. In the past I have been known to find a second gear, a shifty move, a surge of strength I didn't know I had. And sometimes I have failed to find these things, and the other man has taken me down. But not this time. I was running as fast as I know how and then I hit the breaks real sudden, just enough to cause the cornerback's eyes and brain to tell him to pull up short, even though the rest of his body wanted to finish the run at full speed and knock me into the table on the sidelines with all the cups of Gatorade that would go flying in the air. That was all I needed, that one little disturbance in the cornerback's brain-body connection. I took a step to the inside and the man was lost, flailing at my spectral form as momentum drew him like fate toward the Gatorade table.

I crossed the goal line to the roar of the crowd and the shouts of my teammates. Placebo Washington was already in the end zone, laughing and extending a hand for a high-five. Charley Hooks, who'd been running downfield to block, came up behind me and jumped on my back. "Not bad for a white boy!" he yelled.

After the game reporters crowded around Placebo, who'd caught another touchdown pass in the fourth quarter, sealing a 45-13 victory. He held court for a while, then excused himself for a shower so he could get ready for his interview with Cris Colinsworth of HBO.

Colinsworth was already in the locker room, circulating among the players and coaches. When I came out of the shower I saw him chatting with Klaus Kohler. Klaus is a German import, a loud, jovial brute with a thick accent. He reminds me of the guy in

Raiders of the Lost Ark, the bare-chested, bald-headed Nazi who fistfights Indiana Jones because he likes fist-fighting. Klaus is no Nazi, though. Like all self-respecting Germans he hates that legacy. If you made a jocular reference to it you could end up like Ipana Brown, dumped head-first into a laundry hamper.

As I walked past them, Colinsworth looked up and caught my eye, then smiled and shot me a wink. "Nice move, champ," he said.

I stopped and nodded at him. "Thanks."

At that moment Placebo came from the other side of the room, dressed in a purple satin shirt and smelling of cologne so strong that I worried what it might do to his chromosomes. "Lights, camera, action!" he said. Then Placebo and Colinsworth walked out of the room and I went to my locker.

Just as well, I thought, there's no story here.

I wasn't feeling sorry for myself, or cheated in some way because the man from HBO didn't want to sit me down in front of the camera. But I was human and couldn't help thinking how great it would be to have my mug on *Inside the NFL*. No chance of that, though. Colinsworth was doing a story about an up-and-comer who might make it to the big-time. Nobody wanted to watch a segment about a guy who never made it and wasn't about to.

I was dressing and Kenny Liebowitz decided to come over and chew my ear off. "Pretty good-looking guy, you know?"

"Colinsworth?"

"Yeah."

"You interested?" I slipped into my shirt, a sky-blue button-down from Brooks Brothers. It would have made a nice impression on TV.

Kenny changed the subject. "Think they'll show your play on HBO?"

"What? Hell, no. Why would they? The segment's about Placebo."

"Yeah, but they might have an intro. Thirty seconds on this new league that's growing NFL stars of the future. You never know, Fin. You might get on."

Later that night I found myself considering this possibility while I tossed in my bunk, and I cursed Kenny for putting such a thought in my head. NFL Films and HBO were for guys like Peyton Manning and Terrell Owens and Tiki Barber. Not Fin Connors. No fucking way.

I took some comfort in reminding myself how much I dislike the narration that accompanies the footage shown by NFL Films. It's way too serious. You have to ask, what are we watching here, a football game, or the siege of Stalingrad? The narrator—and it's always the same guy—has a terrific vice, sure. But he could lighten up a little. Or maybe they could give the job to Drew Carey.

I was getting in deep not just with Laura, but with Cody, too. When I came over we'd go in the yard to play Frisbee or have a catch with a football. At seven o'clock we'd watch the Three Stooges on AMC while Laura, happy to escape, did the dinner dishes. Cody was a big Stooges fan. I'm more of a Laurel & Hardy guy, but the Stooges make me smile most of the time. If Cody had a friend over, the place would be filled with their laughter at all the goofy slapstick. With Cody guiding me, I became a Stooge scholar, paying close attention to the nuances of eye-poking, face-slapping, and that weird thing with the vibrating hand that goes up and down, hypnotically forcing the watcher to move his head in concurrence with the hand until his face is slammed into a table top. I noted the recycled plots, occurring first in episodes from the thirties and forties, and later in those with Shemp, the poor man's Curly.

Cody taught me things about the Stooges I might never have noticed. Once we were watching a feature film, *Snow White and the Three Stooges,* and there came a scene in which Prince Charming and Snow White burst into song (while the Stooges lurked nearby in the bushes). Cody snorted in disgust. "The Stooges don't have time for singing," he said. Of course they didn't. How could they sit still for a song when there were eyes to be poked, toes to be stomped, dubious missions to be carried out in frantic haste? After watching an episode in which Curly had an especially rough time from Moe, being tweaked and slapped and squirted with seltzer, Cody said, "Curly doesn't know any better. He just lets people torment him." It occurred to me then that anyone caught in the snare of victim-hood would do well to observe Curly and heed this child's wisdom.

Laura saw how close we were growing and mentioned it one night as we lounged on her feather mattress. Fin," she said, "Cody really likes you a lot."

"Doesn't everyone?"

"No, I mean it. Yesterday he told me that he loves you."

"Is that bad?"

Laura sat up and turned to face me. "It could be. Let's be honest."

I was quiet. I felt Laura's eyes burning into me. This, I knew, was a moment that could turn things sour in a hurry. Up to this point everything had been sweet. We dated and had sex. We sat on her couch and watched TV and did things with Cody, like we were a family. Now that sense of being a family was challenged by what we had not said to each other, by what we had not openly considered. Our possible future, or lack of one.

"Well," I said, "it's not a bad thing at all, because I love Cody back. And I love you, too. Sorry if I haven't made that clear." Such a romantic I am.

Her eyes filled. Her face softened. She smiled, tears welling in her eyes. Always the tears with this gender. "I love you, too," she

234

said, and then buried her beautiful wet face into my shoulder.

Although I disliked leaving Laura's warm bed late at night, I welcomed the fifteen-minute drive in the car, alone, the radio silent, my mind working on the problems and choices life was dumping in my lap.

Okay, so we'd gone and said it. Now we would have to deal with the idea of commitment. And monogamy. And perhaps in a year or so we'd talk about getting engaged. And if we liked the idea, after another year had flown by—or maybe two or three—we could tie the knot.

I had to smile. This line of thought was obviously scaring the crap out of me. I was planning a nice long engagement. But that was unrealistic. Hell, it was time to be an adult.

For one thing, I was already thinking of Cody as my own son. His father never visited, never wrote, and anyway to me blood means very little. How big a deal can it be to produce a child? Don't millions of guys do that every day? They hump away and blow a wad that carries the genetic code to produce another loser just like themselves. Then they call the kid Junior because they have to remind everyone that the kid came from their scrotum and not from somebody else's, like it would matter. The only thing that matters, in my opinion, is how you treat the kid. The only thing that counts is loving the kid and letting him be what he's meant to be, even if it's something that doesn't mesh with your big plans to sire the next Nolan Ryan or an heir worthy to step into your shoes as CEO of Shitforbrains Ltd.

If I sound bitter, I guess it's because I've seen too many dads boast about the kid when it's easy, when the boy hits one out of the park or the girl sings solo in the school play. And then Dad disappears when it's time to sit down and go over homework or buy new clothes for school. I know what I'm talking about. My dad was a laugh riot, a flush-faced loveable Irishman who would show us off to his cronies at the bar, but didn't love us enough to keep a steady job.

All a kid wants is to be cared for. This I learned as a camp counselor. I had a camper named Glen Wilson, a tough kid who was funny but gave no quarter. An eleven-year-old hard ass. I remember playing in a doubles tournament with him as my partner. It was counselor-kid vs. counselor-kid. We won the match when Glen smashed a volley into the groin of counselor Mick Duncan, a soccer-playing ruffian from the streets of Glasgow. Duncan collapsed and lay like a fetus, clutching his mashed testicles as the pain slowly grew to that sickening crescendo guys know only too well. One's immediate impulse was to tender aid, to ask if he was okay. Glen ran around the net and crouched next to Duncan. I thought he was going to apologize. But instead the little pisser put his hand flat on his own face, fingers spread open so it looked like the spidery larval creature from *Alien*—the well-known *In your face!* gesture. Everyone watching laughed their asses off while Glen hustled into the woods to hide from Mick.

Once I came back to camp after a day off in town and learned that Glen was in the infirmary with a fever. Nothing serious, but they wanted to keep him overnight. After I helped my co-counselor put the kids to bed, I hiked up to the infirmary to see how Glen was doing. The camp nurse was on the screened porch playing cards with a friend. The night was warm and still, full of insect ratcheting. I walked into the semi-dark room where they kept the patients, usually one or two kids, more often nobody at all. At first I thought Glen was asleep. A comic book lay open at the foot of the bed. But I heard the slithery sound of his pajamas against the sheets as he sat up.

"Hi, Fin," he said. He sounded pretty animated for a sleepy kid with a fever.

"What's the scam?" I said. "You got a fever like I got courtside tickets to the Knicks-Lakers." Even in the dark I could tell he was smiling.

"I dunno. I felt kinda sick after dinner. I feel better now."

I put my hand on his forehead. It *did* feel a little warm. "I get it. You want the nurse to come in here and give you an alcohol rub-down, right?"

Glen made a face. I didn't blame him. The nurse went about two-forty, and she wasn't jolly.

"Why'd you come to see me?" asked Glen. There was an odd note of sincerity to his voice. I wasn't used to hearing it from this lit-

238

tle wise-ass. I shrugged. "I just wanted to check on you. Kids die up here all the time, you know. Last year it was an outbreak of leprosy. I guess they didn't put that in the brochures."

Glen laughed. He asked me what I'd done on my day off. He talked about an upcoming baseball game with a neighboring camp, and wondered if he could be the lead-off hitter, because if he got to first he could steal second and even third before they'd know what hit them. He complained about the rotten food in the dining hall, and said that he and Brad Forsythe had definitely seen a bear, or the hindquarters of one, at least, during last week's nature hike, even though everyone said they were lying.

After a while I had to go. "You need anything?" I asked. "Something to drink? More comics?"

"I'm okay," said Glen. "Actually I'm pretty tired."

I got up to leave.

"Hey, Fin," he said, "thanks for coming to see me."

I narrowed my eyes like Clint Eastwood. "Anytime, punk."

Next day Glen was fine, back to his normal hellion self. But in the remaining weeks of camp I saw a change in his attitude toward me. We'd always gotten along just fine, even when I was threatening to hang him by his thumbs from a rafter. But now I sensed real warmth. He sought me out for conversation that moved beyond the usual banter. Once when he was crying on the night after Parents' Day, he asked me to sit with him on his bunk for a while. He wouldn't say what had made him cry, and I didn't push. I just sat with him quietly and felt the warm breeze coming off the lake through the cabin window, and when he slumped over I put him under the covers. I knew his home situation wasn't great, but other than the fact of him being a rich kid, there weren't a lot of details. But I did know that Glen had been touched by my visit to the infirmary, something I hadn't given much thought to at the time.

So I knew about kids. They wanted to give you unconditional love. All they needed was an opening.

When I walked in the dorm, the guy at the desk said there was a message for me. I looked at the writing on the yellow post-it note: Your brother Kevin will arrive tomorrow.

On my way to the TV room I crumpled the paper and tossed it in a wastebasket. It was only a little past eleven. I hoped nobody was playing video games or watching a Jackie Chan movie. I needed a diversion. And I was in luck. A bunch of the guys were lounging about watching *Personal Best,* a film about a women's collegiate track team. I had seen it before and was eager to see it again. I plopped down on the sofa next to Paul Facemeyer, who had his arms folded and his eyes shut and his mouth half-open in a faint snore. I'd come in at just the right moment, when female crotches, one after the other, were going up and over the high-jump bar in slow motion. When the scene was done, Neal Zank said, "This is a great movie."

I watched for a while but couldn't keep my mind on the action. I was still in my own head, sorting things out and worrying. Kevin and I hadn't spoken in many months, and that was okay. Kevin tends to lose himself in his life and forget about his brother back east. I don't take it personally. But why would he be traveling all the way from Oregon? Thanksgiving was near, but Kevin never gave a damn about holidays. I figured it had to be something with mom, who would not call me even though I was four hours away by car. Mom and I have never gotten along much, but hell, I would be there if she needed me. The more I thought about it, the more pissed I got. I left before the movie was over. Went upstairs and did my ablutions and climbed into bed.

I thought about Kevin, who had always been a little strange. I was two years older and had tried to look out for him, not an easy task. You never knew what he was up to. Somewhere among my papers I had a drawing Kevin had done when he was in the third grade at St. Thomas Aquinas School. It showed St. Lawrence being roasted alive on a spit. The nuns had been reading the class tales of the martyrs, and when Kevin learned that St. Lawrence had been dubbed the patron saint of humor because he'd made a wisecrack while enduring death by fire, he'd been knocked out. It's a damn good piece of work for somebody in the third grade. St. Lawrence's flesh is burned black and smoking. He has a smile on his face and overhead there's a caption that reads, "You can turn me over now, I think I'm done on this side." Roman soldiers are standing around scratching their heads, and up in the clouds Jesus and a bunch of angels are falling all over themselves laughing. The nuns thought it was great.

But his next work of art got him in trouble. He drew the scourging of Jesus, and it was just too gruesome. The image of Christ chained to the pillar, his bowed head a swamp of thorns and blood-drenched hair, one eye dangling from its socket, made a nun cry. When the Mother Superior pillaged his desk to locate any similarly evil-minded drawings, a cache of *Famous Monsters of Filmland* magazines was found. From that day on he was an outcast.

By the time he got to high school he'd figured out it was best to keep his opinions to himself. He drifted through, biding his time, attracting little attention. It helped that his older brother was a standout athlete. The jocks who normally might have enjoyed beating him up because he was different held back out of respect for me.

In college, everything changed. Kevin easily established himself with a group of friends who did art and wrote poetry and played music and reveled in the taking of drugs. We were at the same college and I made a point of hanging around so I could keep an eye on him. In those days I was mostly a pot-smoking, beer-guzzling type of guy. I'd taken a couple of acid trips that convinced me I was a character in a cosmic odyssey, but when I came down I decided that reality, or the appearance of reality, was interesting enough without the acid. Downs—seconals, tuinals, even some dilaudid a teammate scored once from the medicine cabinet of a dying grandmother—filled me with the perfect knowledge that the world was a beautiful and comforting place where all I had to do was lie back and smile and nothing would ever bother me again. Until the next day when I dragged myself to football practice wondering who had poured concrete into my legs while I was passed out. Speed was out of the question. It gave me the sweats, the shits, and perpetual foaming at the corners of my mouth. Cocaine was in the same dangerous category. Sure, it could generate mind-blowing orgasms—

something I learned first-hand during a night of line-snorting and languorous fucking with a sensuous blonde—but it was far too dangerous to fool with. The memory of a mind-blowing orgasm wouldn't matter when you'd lost all your money, your self-respect, your soul. George Carlin said it best. Someone asked him what cocaine makes you feel like, and he said it makes you feel like doing more cocaine. These days I don't do anything, not even pot, which for some reason makes me jittery and worried. I guess it's my time in life to be straight.

But back then I allowed myself to have some fun while playing the solicitous big brother. Kevin rented a small house with three other guys, including the notorious Jack Frye, also known as Dr. Dramamine. They called him that because he loved to get high on Dramamine, an over-the-counter motion sickness pill that contained an extract of the datura plant. Jack insisted that a motion sickness pill was required for the bumpy rides on Orange Sunshine that transported him to Alpha Centauri and beyond, and that the rigors of such a trip demanded swallowing not the prescribed one or two tabs, but the whole package. Datura, he explained to me in one of his rare lucid moments, had been taken by medieval witches, and induced astral projection and sensations of flying. In fact, he continued, those witches would grease broom handles with datura butter and use them for dildos, hence the common, but cleaned-up image of the witch riding her broom across the night sky. And notice she's always smiling, said Jack. I was pleased to see that even though Jack was a complete fuck-up in the classroom, he *had* managed a little scholarly reading on the side. I believed there was no harm in occasionally altering one's consciousness, and in a moment of weakness I ate a handful of Dramamine and waited with Jack for the onset of flying and astral projection. Jack said I should flavor the experience with Orange Sunshine, but I didn't think so. Later I would regret not taking it; I didn't see how the experience could have been any worse than it was. It began with sudden rushes that felt like electric current passing through my vital organs. Then came a sense of foreboding, like the fall of endless night. I came to realize that pot paranoia was like sitting on a porch swing

246

with grandpa, compared to Dramamine psychosis with sinister Lovecraftian ghouls waiting to leap out at you from hidden dimensions. And flying? Yes, there was flying, but I wasn't doing it. It was the furniture. I remember thinking—even in the midst of panic—"What a curious hallucination!" First the electric rush would come, and then a chair or a bookcase would hurl itself at me while I screamed in terror. It was the kind of bummer where I begged God for help and was immediately attacked by a kitchen table.

I learned my lesson, and from that terrible night on did nothing heavier than a doobie.

The days of fun ended one afternoon during a wild party. The house was filled with drunk, tripping people bellowing at each other to be heard above the absolutely cranked Led Zeppelin. In his bedroom Kevin was holding a nude séance with three lovely Theater Arts majors. (Sorry, he said, to male intruders. Girls only. Sappho would not appear if there were naked guys present. He didn't count, being the medium.) I was in the living room savoring a beer and a joint when the landlord came in through the front door.

He was Mr. Farnetti, a retired barber. He had a brother-in-law who was a town cop. Calmly, Mr. Farnetti observed the goings-on. A howling came from the kitchen. Mr. Farnetti went in to investigate. I stubbed the joint in an ashtray and followed.

Jack Frye was supine on the floor, underneath the open door of the refrigerator. His head was tilted so he could see what was going on inside the fridge. A couple of his buddies were rearranging the bottles of ketchup and mustard, a package of hot dogs, the butter, the beer. The combination of chemicals Jack had taken caused him to believe that the contents of the fridge were in fact the contents of his brain. With each shifting of objects he would release a howl that became maniacal laughter, because, as he later told it, it was scary but also cosmically hilarious to have people messing— literally—with his brain.

Mr. Farnetti remained composed. He extended a hand and helped the dazed boy to his feet. Patiently he explained that the neighbors had complained about the noise, and so the music must be turned down. In addition, he said, Jack and his roommates would have to leave the premises by the end of the month, which, he was happy to point out, was only a week in coming.

Kevin graduated on time and had to find a job. He could draw and paint pictures and write interesting poetry, and of course none of this made him special in the world of work. Debbie and I gave him some cash to buy a pair of wingtips for job interviews. On his way to Thom McCann he saw a globe of the world in the window of a department store, and he bought it with the wingtip money. That night when Debbie was finished yelling at him (I just sat and watched, no point in doing anything else), Kevin explained that it made more sense to buy the globe because it was something he'd always wanted. For a couple of years he drifted from one menial job to another. Then he connived his way into a graduate program at Syracuse. He applied himself, got a Masters in Comparative Arts, and then, to the amazement of all his friends and family, went ahead and completed the Ph.D. Now he taught art at a small college in Oregon. Why he was coming east I didn't know, but I would find out soon enough.

Kevin showed up at the end of practice. I was at my locker un-taping a knee that had been giving me some trouble. I looked up and there he was, grinning down at me. I hadn't seen him in four years. He was over thirty now, but seemed younger. When people see us together they know we're brothers, but Kevin, I must admit, is better looking. At six-two he's half an inch taller than me, and at one-eighty-five he's thirty pounds lighter, which means he looks more elegant in street clothes. He has thicker hair, a smaller nose, a leaner face. My eyes are cesspool gray, his are Neptunian green. That's what he tells people when I'm in earshot, just to piss me off. Although it was November and cold outside, he wore no hat or overcoat. His Harris Tweed jacket looked brand new, unlike the ancient tie, red with purple lozenges, a rummage sale find. I stood up and we hugged.

Middle linebacker Joe Mankowski had the locker next to mine. When he saw the embrace he coughed loudly, yelling "Faggot!" at the same time. It was the old joke from *Animal House*. "Relax," I said. "This is my brother."

Kevin extended his hand. "But we're still fags," he said. I made a few introductions and Kevin charmed everyone with his bright smile and open, friendly manner. He'd come a long way from being the reclusive high school bizarro.

I continued to undress. "So what's up?"

"Take your shower," said Kevin. "We'll talk at dinner."

I drove us to an *Outback*. The steaks there are pretty good, and I had a craving for a blooming onion. On the way I pressed Kevin to tell me why he had come.

"It's mom," he said. "She's dying."

Of course I knew that's what it had to be. I said nothing. My face started to feel hot. I kept my eyes on the road. "I find this out from you?"

"I know it's weird," said Kevin, "but what can you say? She is what she is. You shouldn't take it personal."

I laughed. "So how should I take it? *Impersonal*? That make it any better?"

We drove on in silence. Snow began falling, light flakes so delicate they melted on contact with the windshield. I turned on the wipers. "What is it? Cancer?"

"I'm afraid so. It's her lungs. Doctor says she has two or three months."

Our mother had always looked good. Pretty, never fat. Kept her hair long even after it started to go gray in her forties. A never-say-die hippie, she wore colorful bandanas and hoop earrings and skirts and blouses that looked like they'd been woven and dyed in the land of the Himalayas. But a lifetime of chain smoking Camels had made her smell like a Shriner's poker night, even though she moved through clouds of incense and dabbed patchouli oil on her wrists. She had the fog-horn voice of someone who smokes too many cigarettes or drinks too much whiskey. In her case it was both. With such people booze and tobacco run neck and neck to see which can do the killing first. Tobacco had won. She was fifty-nine and wouldn't make it to sixty.

We pulled into the packed parking lot, made our way into the warm and clattery steakhouse and were shown to a table. I had some trouble concentrating on the menu, eventually settled on a basic steak platter. Kevin got the G'day Mate Plate, which came with a blooming onion. At his request I helped him pick at it, but without much appetite. Before the food proper arrived we talked of the depressing business ahead. Debbie was already there, he said. She'd flown in from San Diego last week. She would stay till the end and handle the hospital stuff, the legal stuff, all of it. Mom didn't have a house or much money. For years she'd messed around in telemarketing and sales clerking. Fortunately she'd landed a job with a caterer that did quite well in the Boston suburbs. Their medical plan would provide the necessary care.

I took a sip from my water glass. "Why didn't Debbie call me?"

"She only found out a few days ago. She's been running around like a headless chicken, taking care of her own business long distance."

I shook my head in disgust. "Am I such a bad son, a bad brother? What the fuck did I do that nobody tells me anything?"

"This isn't about you, Fin."

"Easy for you to say. Mom always liked you best," I said, evoking a Smothers Brothers routine our dad used to play for us on his old turntable.

Kevin barely smiled. "She loves you as much as she loves anyone."

"Which is to say not very deeply."

Kevin chose not to reply. Our steaks came. The smell of charred flesh activated my taste buds and stomach juices. Mom was dying, but I had to eat. In silence we stabbed and chewed. I ate most of my steak and baked potato, then rejected dessert offers from the perky waitress. I drained my glass of ice water and picked up the tab. Kevin objected, but this was my town.

Kevin was staying the night at the Marriott Courtyard Inn. When he traveled he wanted a good bed, peace and quiet, more security than provided by a motel on the street where thugs could pull up right in front of your window, mere feet away from where you twitched and perspired in half-sleep on a sagging mattress.

We sat in his room for a while talking and glancing at TV. Kevin removed a joint from his travel kit and fired it up. He held it out to share.

"All yours," I said.

Kevin exhaled bluish billowing smoke and raised his eyebrows. "Since when?"

"Hell, I don't know. A year, maybe?"

"Any particular reason?" He put the joint to his lips and sucked hard.

The hempy, burning smell was wonderful. Top quality bud from the Bigfoot-haunted forests of the Northwest Territory. Maybe I'd ask him to leave me a sample. A few months from now I might have a different attitude.

"Not really," I said. "It just stopped feeling right."

Kevin watched me through the haze of smoke. "You don't drink anymore, you told me that."

"Not a drop. Well, practically not a drop."

"Nothing else? No coke, ecstasy?"

"Are you nuts? Look, I don't do anything."

He drummed the fingers of his free hand on the glossy faux mahogany desk provided by the Marriott Corporation. "Cigarettes are out. I'm sure of that." His face suddenly brightened. "Coffee!"

I shook my head. "Not a big fan. Sometimes in the morning, when I really need it."

Kevin stared at me. The smoke from the joint he held between his thumb and index

255

rose to the ceiling in a thick stream. "Don't you realize how boring you are?"

I laughed. "What about chocolate? I have a little chocolate maybe every day."

"*Chocolate?* Fin, let me tell you, *guys* don't get hooked on chocolate."

I looked at the TV. An old favorite was coming on. "Let's drop it, son. Anyway, the pot's kicking in. You won't be able to make complete sentences in another minute or two."

So we watched *Cheers,* the funny-sad story of Sam and Diane, the same thing played out between lovers everywhere, just about every time. Desire, hope, then loss. All of this—the show, sitting in a hotel room with my stoned brother, the news of our mother's illness, the raw cold night that would soon swallow me alive—made me feel very tired. I sat in a functional easy chair thinking how pleasant it would be if I never had to move again, if my body and the chair would suddenly fuse and turn to stone, leaving me placidly smiling and Buddha-like, feeling nothing, resting for eternity.

"I gotta go," I said, rising from the chair with difficulty.

Kevin got up off the bed and hugged me. "See you next week, right? After Thanksgiving?"

"Sure," I said. "I'll be there."

The Scranton Miners had a secret. The best player in their secondary, Waylon Grooms, was narcoleptic. There was videotape from his college days at Texas Lutheran, so it wasn't as if nobody in the world had ever known this. The tape showed Grooms running stride for stride with a receiver and then, for no apparent reason, collapsing like a bag of mulch while the startled receiver loped onward to haul in the pass. A local paper did an against-all-odds human-interest story on him, but when Grooms went undrafted and unsigned as a free agent, people forgot about his special challenge. In fact, they forgot about him altogether. And a few years later when he surfaced with Scranton in the NFA, nobody remembered.

But our defensive backs coach Tom Patterson received an anonymous letter and a clipping about Grooms. Included with the letter was a magic charm which, when spoken in Grooms' presence, would induce a narcoleptic seizure at once. So said the anonymous letter, at any rate. Patterson figured the writer was Grooms' ex wife or girlfriend, out for revenge, and was about the toss the letter into the wastebasket when he hesitated. Why *not* use an advantage, if it really existed. He brought the letter into Lou's office. I was there at the time, talking with Lou about some problems with the wideouts. Lou read the letter carefully, then looked up at Patterson. "Tempted?"

Patterson shifted in his chair. With one word, uttered in a mildly sarcastic tone, Lou had kicked the legs out from under him. "Maybe a little. But that's crazy, isn't it?"

"Certifiably." Lou lifted the lid off the candy dish on his desk and scooped out a handful of M&Ms. "Not that I don't understand the attraction. Crazy ideas are fun." He indicated the candy dish. "Help yourself." Patterson declined.

"The thing is," said Lou, meticulously removing all the red M&Ms from the batch he held in his hand, "there are three excellent reasons not to buy into this. Number one, it's unethical. Number two, it probably wouldn't work. And number three, if it ever got out that we tried this cockamamie bullshit, we'd be the laughing stock of the league." He tossed the remaining M&Ms into his mouth.

Patterson nodded. "I agree. It was just a thought." He couldn't take his eyes from the red M&Ms lined up on the desk. "Tell me, Lou. What's so different about the red ones?"

"That's my business," said Lou.

So Patterson balled up the letter and tossed it in the trash. But he made the mistake of telling a couple of players about the letter, because next day the story was all over the locker room. And the letter had been retrieved and unballed. Several players on the offense knew the incantation by heart. Now, a week later, as the Cossacks were ready to take the field against Scranton, Lou felt the need to address the team.

"It has come to my attention," he said, "that some of you are planning to weave a magic spell against Waylon Grooms." There was a low ripple of laughter. "As I gaze upon your simple faces, I understand how appealing this must seem to you." More laughter. "But as your leader, I'm afraid I cannot allow you to practice the black arts on my watch." Groans of mock disappointment.

Coach Gargano chimed in. "Anyway, Grooms is white. Whoever heard of a white guy falling for this juju shit?"

This caused an uproar. Blacks and whites got after each other. I sat back and watched the fun. Finally Lou raised his hand and called for silence. It was time for the Cossacks to put on their game faces.

Scranton was no pushover. We struck first, scoring two touchdowns in the opening quarter, but the Miners came roaring back. They had a wideout named Shiv Saunders who caught two long bombs for touchdowns, and at the half it was fourteen-all. Nobody scored in the third quarter, and then with four minutes left in the game, a very strange thing happened.

We had the ball on our own 41. On third and eight, Darvis Childs ran a slant over the middle and found himself in single coverage. The man covering him was Waylon Grooms. Drew Danielson put the ball in Childs' breadbasket. It was enough yardage for a first down, but that would be all. Grooms, who was having a good night, was closing fast and would make the tackle.

But he didn't make the tackle. He fell face down on the turf and Childs ran all the way to the end zone. When Childs got to the sideline he swore to Lou that he hadn't said a word to Grooms, never mind a magic spell. Later, film of the play would back him up; Grooms could clearly be seen catching his cleats in a loose divot. There had been no sorcery afoot, although everyone on the Cossacks thought it a damned peculiar coincidence that Grooms had fallen just as suddenly as he would have if the charm had been cast.

On Thanksgiving eve the Cossacks dismantled Hartford's powerful offensive machine. Luther Moffitt had a big night with three sacks and a fumble recovery. Watching him play, I had to wonder how he'd been overlooked by NFL scouts. He got after the quarterback like a leopard chasing down a gazelle. His sacks kept Hartford deep in their own territory, and every time they punted we would take the ball so far up field it felt like we could fox trot our way into the end zone. After a fourth quarter field goal and an unanswered touchdown—a 19-yard strike to Placebo Washington—we were coasting along 27-16. We had the ball on our own 35 and Drew handed off three times in a row to Ray Whipple. With less than three minutes left in the game, it was ground control time. On the third carry, Ray saw the hole in front of him start to fill up with the wide posteriors of flailing offensive linemen, so he took it outside the tackle and found some daylight. A tired linebacker threw his arms around him with all the intensity of a mother-in-law's obligatory hug, and Ray broke free. It was clear sailing, nobody close enough to bring him down, but still Ray thought he should switch the ball to his outside arm—the one facing the sideline—in case a speedy defender caught up with him and tried to pop it loose. In a move that would subsequently make the NFA's blooper film, Ray fumbled the ball into open space. It bounced off his knee and rocketed toward the center of the field. A safety who'd been chasing Ray without much enthusiasm now came to life. He grabbed the ball neatly and turned in the opposite direction. Ray had fallen and gotten up again and now was in desperate, despairing pursuit. The safety zigzagged through the chaos of players with suddenly reversed roles—defensive end blocking, the quarterback angling for a tackle—until Charley Hooks tripped him up at the 9.

Hartford took it in for six, but it didn't much matter. We smothered the onside kick and Drew took a knee three times and that was it. What did matter, I knew, was Ray. It was his second fumble in two games. He wasn't running well, wasn't concentrating. His personal problems were getting to him, but he didn't want to discuss it, not even with his old pal.

On a seeing-your-breath cold day, under a gunmetal gray sky, I drove to Laura's house for Thanksgiving. Three inches of wet snow had fallen overnight, and the streets were a stew of slush and salty grit. I couldn't drive ten feet without splashing huge streaks of dirty slush onto the windshield. Even with the wipers going it looked like somebody was washing a dog on the roof of my car.

I went up to the door with a smile on my face and a bouquet of roses in my hand. Laura's older sister was there—Janice, a tall, loose-jointed woman with an ample bottom and a willingness, it turned out, to laugh at all of my jokes. After devouring enormous helpings of turkey, stuffing, mashed potatoes, and Brussels sprouts, all of it swimming in thick, rich gravy, I repaired to the sofa to watch the Lions-Packers game and try not to fall asleep. Cody appeared with Monopoly. We played cutthroat, and things got loud. I had Boardwalk and Park Place, but nobody landed on them and I was losing my shirt. A bad roll of the dice brought me to Marvin Gardens, where Cody had a hotel. When he checked the deed and saw how much rent I had to pay, he was jubilant. "Fork it over," he said. "And make it snappy. I'm a busy man." (While playing the game he talked like all the tough businessmen he'd seen foreclosing on widows in cartoons and old movies.) When I gathered up my fortune and held it out to him, Cody looked confused.

"I don't have enough to pay you," I said. "I'm wiped out. You get all my property and what little money I have left."

When Cody realized what this meant— that I wouldn't be playing anymore—some of the joy drained from his face. But then it came right back as he hit on the solution.

"That's okay," he said. "This time it's on the house."

I wanted to hug the boy, but it would have embarrassed him.

On Friday night a bunch of us were sitting in the lounge discussing football and life.

"How come you suppose some ladies like to be spanked?" said Gemini Harper.

"It's all based on psychology," said Kenny Liebowitz. "Chicks want to do it with their fathers, but they can't admit it, not even to themselves. So they ask *you* for a spanking. *Spank me, daddy! Oh, please, I've been a naughty girl!* It's a daddy fantasy."

"That's weird, man. But I ain't sayin' I don't dig it."

"Wassup, Gemini?" asked Luther Moffitt. "You got some pussy wants you to turn her over and paddle her ass?"

"That's part of it," said Drew Danielson. Drew was seated in the center chair, the most coveted position in the room. And he had control of the remote, to boot, and was using it methodically, maddeningly.

"Come on, man," said Taters Delevan, "find something and stay with it."

Drew ignored him, kept flicking. "It's more than a daddy fantasy," he continued. "At a more basic level, it's simply about pain."

"Perhaps in some cases," said Kenny, who had read a few books on psychology.

I knew that Kenny was gearing up for a lecture; I could feel it coming. So I was glad when Bobby Hertzig interrupted.

"I think Drew's right," said Bobby. "Some people like a little pain with their sex."

"And Drew," said Luther, "he like a little sex with his pain."

Everyone laughed at that. Drew smiled. He gave up the search for something terrific and settled on SportsCenter. Drew was hard to know, and there were some odd rumors about him. It was said that he had a taste for hookers he could tie up with silk scarves and beat with a riding crop. Powerfully built and handsome, with a trim mustache and goatee, he radiated an aura of leadership, and now, at thirty-one, he'd found a new lease on his career. His quarterback rating was high, and he was the league leader in touchdown passes. It didn't hurt that he had Placebo Washington racing downfield to snare his long bombs. He was a drag to room with, it was said, because of his compulsive, Felix Ungerish nitpicking, but nobody had a real beef with him. We knew he could take us all the way.

"The sexiest man I ever knew," continued Bobby, "had a wonderfully sadistic streak. He was a landscaper in Palo Alto." He sighed. "My god, the abs on that boy. Anyway, the first night I spent at his place I noticed he had a bunch of instant lottery tickets on his kitchen counter. They were all winners, but the prize areas hadn't been scratched off. I asked him why, and he said he liked not knowing what the amounts were. He could go about his business not knowing if he was richer by two dollars or half a million."

"I couldn't *stand* that!" said Harper.

"He liked to prolong everything," said Bobby. "Sometimes it was too much. Pleasure would turn into pain."

"Sounds delightful," said Neal Zank.

"It don't mean a thing if it ain't got that sting," said Luther.

The attention of all was drawn to the big screen. On SportsCenter a pretty lady was narrating the story of Starr Donovan, an undrafted running back from Ohio Northern who'd shown up at the Bengals' rookie camp and was now averaging almost six yards a carry on his way to a thousand-yard season. It was one of the great mysteries of football, how all-conference studs from powerhouses like Nebraska were drafted in the first round and failed to live up to their bowl performances, spending a year or two on special teams until drifting out of the league. How blazing fast wideouts from the Big East made the cover of *Sports Illustrated* but couldn't stick with a team that went 2-14 in the NFL. The Starr Donovans of football were flukes, but they did happen. No one, not the savviest scout or general manager, could predict whether a kid had all of what it takes to make it in the pros. Raw talent wasn't enough. You needed smarts and the right attitude. It didn't hurt if you'd been raised in a tarpaper, dirt-floor shack by a single mom who worked in a knitting mill so you could have chicken and cornbread on Sundays. But even that wasn't a guarantee. You might take a fat chunk of your signing bonus and buy your mom a house in the suburbs, because you couldn't even think of what she'd done for you without having tears well up in your eyes. Or you might blow the bulk of it on cars and women and fancy jewelry. There was no telling in advance. Your character would reveal itself under the bright lights and the clamor of the media, and you would find out how strong you were not just in your arms and legs, but in your heart.

One thing was certain. A team didn't have a prayer of knowing who to draft first unless the scouts had done their research, which meant going to a prospect's games and practices, talking to his coaches and teachers, and breaking bread with his family members. You couldn't figure this stuff out from your sofa. I remember watching ESPN's draft coverage one flu-ridden, lost weekend. The draft was held in New York, and the gallery was crowded with Jet and Giant fans dressed in team jerseys. As the Jets prepared to make their first selection, the camera settled on a soft-bodied sad sack in a Jet jersey, holding his hands together in supplication, eyes closed, teeth clenched in anxiety. The slip of paper bearing the name of the Jet pick was delivered to the podium, and Commissioner Tagliabue announced the name of the player who Jet management hoped would lift the team out of its perennial miseries. Apparently it was the player this sad sack had been hoping for. He punched the air with his fists and looked heavenward and said (I could read his lips clearly), *Thank you, God!*

But really, what did that schlub know about football? Two years later he might very well be cursing the name of the player he was now praising to the heavens. Such was often the fate of scouts and general managers, who would gnash their teeth over the blue-chipper who had revealed himself, amid the faster, tougher competition of the NFL, to be a penny stock. Risks aside, I coveted the job of an NFL scout. I'd been playing the game for twenty years now, and I have an eye for talent. Surely one of the teams would hire me. Sitting there in the lounge, I began to daydream of a company car and an expense account.

"Hey, Fin."

Luther Moffitt was calling me. I hadn't been listening.

"Fin! Pay attention, man. We wanna hear about the worst gross-out you ever seen."

So that was it. A common diversion among athletes was to trade tales of the most disgusting, stomach-churning behavior they had ever had the misfortune to witness. The dump somebody took on a coach's birthday cake. The three hundred pound barmaid with her period that a drunken cowboy had gone down on. I had seen plenty like this. And the absolutely worst thing I ever saw I would not repeat, because in the telling I would remember it vividly enough to make me vomit. Instead I told the gang about a prick I knew in college who hated his roommate so much that he secretly stuck the guy's toothbrush up his asshole. This was done in the presence of others, all of whom made sure they were around when the roommate decided to brush his teeth that night. Great fun. I had heard this story second hand. I believe that if I had been there when the creep buried the toothbrush up his butt, I would have thrown it in the trash and told the man if he ever did anything like that again, I would break his nose. Anyway, there was an epilogue to the story and I told it now.

"One of the most fucked-up guys I ever knew," I said, "was Jared Huntoon, this lineman I played with out in California. One day when Jared and I were tippling a few, I told

271

him the toothbrush story. He thought it was so funny he literally fell of his barstool. Then—and I couldn't fucking believe this—he took a notebook out of his backpack and wrote it down. I looked over his shoulder and there it was: *someone you don't like—stick toothbrush up asshole.*"

"Jee-zus!" said Harper.

"I know. I like to think that Jared Huntoon and the other guy will end up roommates in hell."

Neal Zank turned in his chair and faced Luther Moffitt. "Luther, goddammit, put away that notebook!"

Given the nature of the conversation, there was a consensus that now was a good time for yet another viewing of *Outpicks,* a special videotape Cris Collinsworth had given to Ellis Barry, our backfield coach and a former college teammate of Collinsworth's. It showed athletes, coaches, announcers, and other celebrities picking their noses when they didn't know the camera was on them. It seemed like someone was going into Barry's room once a week and borrowing the tape to show in the lounge. Collinsworth loved to pass out copies of the tape because it showed

his buddy and FOX co-analyst Terry Brad-
shaw in full pick during a commercial break.
But the real crowd pleaser was a two-minute
segment of a famous talk show maven digging deep into her nostrils while viciously
browbeating her underlings. You couldn't
help busting a gut to see this icon of daytime
TV burrowing for boogers and screaming at
some hapless gofer, *"Where's my fucking
sandwich?"*

As Coy Jessup was leaving to get the tape,
I decided I wouldn't mind missing the four-
teenth encore presentation of *Outpicks*.

In my room I fluffed up my pillow,
cracked the window a little for fresh air,
turned on my low-wattage reading lamp and
settled into bed with a book. It was only 9:30,
but I felt dog-tired. It couldn't have been
more than ten minutes before the words
stopped making sense. I killed the light and
dropped into the bliss of sleep.

I awoke to a heavy banging on my door. I had
forgotten to lock it, so after a respectful second or two Carthage Lee came barging in.
"Wake up, Fin. We got trouble."

I sat up in bed, feeling sick the way you do when you're jarred out of a deep sleep by somebody telling you there's trouble. The luminous green numbers on my digital clock read 12:47. "What is it?"

"Some crackers beat the shit out of Whipple."

My clothes were in a heap on the floor. I got up and started dressing. *"Crackers?* In *Centerport?"*

"Crackers, trailer trash, call it what you will, man. Let's go."

Carthage and I hustled downstairs. Luther Moffitt and Klaus Kohler and Placebo Washington were sitting with Ray in the lounge. Ray looked like he'd spent the night standing in for a piñata. One eye was swollen shut, and his lips were cracked and bleeding. There was a cut on his forehead and dried blood on one of his ears. When he saw me he tried to smile. "Got a little drunk," he said.

I noticed he didn't seem drunk now. Nothing like a good beating to sober a man up in a hurry. "What the hell happened?"

Ray shrugged. Even that small movement made him wince. He was holding his sides. I guessed they'd kicked his ribs for him.

"Had a disagreement with a couple of extras from *Deliverance*. They didn't think I should be putting moves on Elly Mae, or whatever the fuck her name was. I tried to reason with 'em. Said I wouldn't mind sloppy seconds after their pet billy goat."

"Always the charmer," I said.

Placebo was on his feet, pacing. "Let's *find* these motherfuckers!"

Klaus turned to me with a death's head smile. "We must fight. It is time to break arms and legs."

"Damn right," said Carthage. "These crackers need to learn you don't fuck with the Cossacks."

I was irritated. Seeing Ray all busted up *did* make me want to go after somebody with a baseball bat, but hadn't Ray asked for it? I was a thirty-five year-old man who had no truck with revenge, especially if it involved a gang of hillbillies with buck knives and shotguns. I would have to be the voice of reason. "So what's the plan? We drive into Dogpatch with guns blazing? What we need to do is get Ray here to a hospital. Maybe call the cops."

The smile faded from Klaus Kohler's face. "No police." He held up a fist the size of a cantaloupe. "We take care of it with *this*."

"And *this*," said Placebo. From the inside pocket of his black sharkskin jacket he withdrew a Walther PPK 9-millimeter automatic. I don't know one gun from another, but that's what it was according to Luther, who confiscated it on the spot, moving his gigantic hand faster than seemed humanly possible. You couldn't take a football away from Placebo that easily, but I guess he hadn't expected Luther's intervention.

There probably would have been some arguing over the gun, but just then we heard Lou Levine's loud, pissed-off voice coming from the doorway. "And what mischief are my babies up to tonight?"

He was in his robe and slippers. His hair was disheveled. He did not look happy. When he saw Ray, his features sagged.

"Hiya, coach," said Ray, giving a jaunty wave and then wincing from the pain.

Lou went to the couch where Ray sat like a dumpling, all the fight gone out of him. He took stock of the bruises and cuts. Then he surveyed the room. "Has there been some thought of taking matters into our own hands?"

Everyone shifted uncomfortably. "A little," I said.

"Maybe a lot," said Luther. "But cooler heads have prevailed."

"That's good," said Lou. He sat down opposite Ray. Sighed heavily and looked at him with sadness. "You look pretty beat up."

"I feel pretty beat up."

"You know me," said Lou. "I like to stay positive at all times. But I'm thinking you might not be ready to play football anytime soon."

Ray stared at the floor. "I'll be ready."

"Okay," said Lou. "Fin, how about you and Luther escort Mr. Whipple to the emergency room. And the rest of you better hit the sack. We have a meeting tomorrow morning, I believe."

Luther and I eased Ray into the back of my Camry. I said maybe Luther would be more useful staying at the dorm. Somebody had to keep an eye on Placebo. Luther agreed.

On the way to the hospital, Ray got a little weepy. "I really fucked up, didn't I? I'm done for the year, and that means for good."

"Let's wait and see how banged up you are."

It was a cold, clear night. Some houses already had Christmas decorations up. Red plastic Santas in the front yards, blue lights in the windows. I could hear a whistle in Ray's breathing. If he had broken ribs, he *was* finished. There were only two games left in the regular season, and ribs don't heal that fast.

"Why'd I do it?" said Ray. "Why couldn't I get through this like a man?"

I snorted. "This is what men do. We get our hearts broken and we fuck up. Five years from now you'll do it again."

Ray laughed, then said *"Ow!"* from the pain. "We were married nine years, Fin. I really loved her. Hell, I only cheated on her twice the whole time we were together."

"You were a good husband, Ray."

"I was damn good. A good father, too." His voice broke. He began sobbing quietly. I clicked on the radio, tried to locate some heavy metal, something to lighten the mood.

But all I could get was commercials, talk shows, a piano concerto. I found some pop, but it turned out to be a painful love song on an oldies station. I turned it off.

"I let her do this to me," said Ray. "She doesn't give a fuck about me, and I kept loving her, kept hoping she'd take me back."

I could hear him sniffling. I thought about tossing a box of Kleenex into the back seat, but that's what you'd do for a woman, and I didn't think Ray would appreciate it. They'd clean the snot off his face along with the blood at the ER.

"You know what, Fin?"

"What?"

"I was going pretty good, wasn't I? Better than anyone expected. I even surprised Lou."

"You still can."

"Sure," said Ray.

I glanced in the rear view mirror. I saw Ray wipe his nose on the sleeve of his jacket and turn to stare out the window. "One good year," he said. "I wasn't burning up the league, but it was a good year. That's all I wanted."

One good year. It doesn't seem like a lot to ask for. But in real life it never happens.

There's no such thing as a whole year that's good. That's why I love football. You can define a whole year by a season. If it's a good season, it stands out like a fat diamond on a showgirl's finger, and all the sorrow and shit that goes on for the rest of the year doesn't matter so much.

We pulled into the hospital parking lot. I led Ray through the automatic sliding doors into the ER. After some formalities, they gave him a hospital gown and had him lie on a gurney in a small examining room. "Mind if I stay?" I asked the nurse. "I had to listen to him cry and moan all the way over here. I think I deserve to watch you stitch him up. No pain-killers, please."

"That's up to the doctor," she said, with no trace of amusement.

When the doctor came he didn't kick me out of the room. He was a small man with a dark complexion and a pencil-thin mustache. His name-tag said he was Dr. Arroyo. He took a couple of minutes to inspect the damage. "What happened to you?"

"Dorm hockey," said Ray.

Dr. Arroyo looked at him impassively.

280

"You play it in the hallway," I offered. "Three on three. It's a rough game."

"You should see the other guys," said Ray.

Ray didn't have any broken ribs. One was slightly cracked. He would miss the next game with Springfield, but might return for the final game at home against Albany. All we had to do was win one more and the Cossacks would play for the Championship.

Lou signed a kid he knew from the city to take Ray's roster spot. Dunnan Bradstreet, 5'10", 205. Like so many, he had a troubled past. Drugs, gangs, two children out of wedlock with two different women. But he was coming around, taking classes at CUNY. He was studying pre-law, but hoped for a stint in the NFL. Playing for the Cossacks in this emergency role could put a shine on his resume.

The night before the team left for Springfield, I went to Lou's office. I told him about my mother's illness, and asked if I could go right from the game to Waltham and spend a couple of days with her. She'd probably still be around after the season was over, but you never knew.

Lou said it was okay. He reached behind his chair, took two bottles of Poland Spring water from a small refrigerator and slid one across the desk. "So when do I get to meet your girlfriend? Laura, right?"

"Laura, yes. I don't know. One of these days."

Lou took a long swig of water, all the while keeping his eyes on me. "You serious about this girl?"

I fiddled with the bottle cap but didn't twist it off. "That's a good question."

Lou looked surprised. "Really? How so? Either you are or you aren't." His smile was a challenge.

I smiled back. "You're always so sure about everything."

Lou gasped theatrically. "Not at all. Just about some things. Look, Fin, you're not a kid anymore. From what you tell me, you've got a nice woman here. What's holding you back?"

I didn't have a ready answer. Lou supplied one. "Fear," he said. "It's at the root of every mistake you'll ever make in your life."

"What's wrong with a little fear?" I said. "Pretty girls make graves."

Lou made a face. "What a load of crap. Sure, it's fun to quote Kerouac, but you know what, Fin? Kerouac was a bum. The great Bodhisattva who loved only himself. Never even gave a shit about his kid."

"All I mean is—"

"I know exactly what you mean. Desire keeps you stuck on the meat wheel. But pretty girls make more than graves. They make your bed warm. They make the moment beautiful. Some of them, at least."

I put the unopened bottle on Lou's desk. "You know what Sal said to me the other day? He comes up to me and he says, 'Hey, kid, I hear you're getting married.' I told him he was crazy, but he ignored me. 'Listen,' he says, 'you remember one thing. Taking care of a woman is a full-time job, and that's capital J-O-B, and that stands for Jewelry, Orgasms, and Babies.'"

Lou smiled. "Sal's a funny guy." He nodded at the bottle on his desk. "You don't want it?"

I got up to leave. "Not thirsty."

The insignia of the Springfield Screaming Homers had been designed by Matt Groening, the creator of *The Simpsons.* Owner Charley Kousaleas had been pondering possible names for the team when his fourteen-year-old son suggested he call them the Homers, after the Simpsons' patriarch. It was fitting, he pointed out, since the Simpsons lived in the town of Springfield. No one knew what state this mythical Springfield was located in, (although in one whimsical episode, Kentucky was named) but it could just as easily be Massachusetts as Illinois or Missouri. Kousaleas had seen the show more than a few times, and when he recalled an episode about football, he knew what the insignia must be: an image of Homer Simpson screaming as he's being kicked through the goalposts.

Kousaleas' lawyers worried that Groening might not be interested in the idea. But when they contacted him for permission they were pleasantly surprised. Not only did he give his okay, he even offered to draw the Screaming Homer. His only stipulation was that half of the profits from T-shirts, mugs, and other accessories bearing the logo be donated to his favorite charity, a fund for the preservation of the flora and fauna of the Pacific Northwest, a very Lisa Simpson-like cause. I couldn't think of anyone on the Cossacks who didn't get a charge out of *The Simpsons*, (with the exception of Hollis Daft, who often suffered comparisons to Flanders, the show's token Christian). The only problem was we weren't going up against Homer and Marge and Smithers and Montgomery C. Burns. Next to Manchester, the Homers were the toughest team we would face. They had a super-charged offense with a platoon of whippet-fast wideouts, led by Earl Dowd, 6'4", 187, a gangly white boy from Idaho who could fly. They had a scrambling quarterback and a 260-pound fullback you had to gang tackle. You couldn't stop the Screaming Homers, you could only hope to slow them down a little.

And that's what we did, matching them score for score until the last quarter. Then, with 8:18 left in the game and Springfield marching down the field, Joe Mankowski intercepted a tipped pass and we had the ball on our own 40. Seven minutes later, after an elegant drive orchestrated by Drew Danielson, highlighted by his pinpoint passes to six different receivers, and capped by Dunnan Bradstreet's two-yard sweep around left end for the score, we had the lead, 42-35. The Screaming Homers had one more shot but couldn't pull the trigger. On fourth and three with 21 seconds left in the game, Coy Jessup sacked the quarterback at midfield, and it was all over.

We would play Manchester in the Championship game.

I drove east toward Boston, a trip I had made many times before. In the summer the turnpike was a pleasant ride. But not in December, with low clouds and a steady drizzle of cold rain. I wasn't in the mood for music, so I killed time by counting hawks. You can always depend on seeing plenty of hawks on the Mass pike, especially in sour weather. They sit in trees, waiting for rabbits and rodents to appear in the wet weeds below. It must be miserable for them, soaked and hungry, perched in the raw cold. But they sit and wait. What choice do they have?

I counted fifteen hawks and then started thinking about my mother. Probably this would be the last time I'd see her alive. I had the standard feelings, but they were tainted by bitterness. There had never been a lot of warmth flowing out of Trish to her kids. Her friends loved the hell out of her, though. She was always popular, always had her nose in some cause or activity. But if you woke up in the night puking on your pajamas, there was no tenderness in her ministrations. She would tell you to get in the damn shower and clean yourself off. There'd be a fresh pair of pajamas waiting for you when you emerged wet and shaking from the bathroom, and she'd be sitting on the edge of your bed with a bottle of medicine and a spoon, but the look on her face told you all you needed to know about what a pain in the ass you were to be getting sick at this ungodly hour.

Trish wasn't funny like dad. She didn't *say* funny things. I don't remember her ever getting off a good comeback. But she was often fun. She knew how to have a good time, baking cookies while she sang and danced around the room, or chasing us kids down the sidewalk with a water pistol. I would never say she was a bad person, not at all. She just didn't seem to care a whole lot about what was going on inside the heads and hearts of her own children.

This had not been such a problem for Kevin. He once told me he would have felt uncomfortable if his own mother knew what he was all about. Going deep was for his pals, and for the women he slept with, though not all of them, he hastened to add.

Debbie was more like me. She figured a mother and daughter should be soul mates. When Debbie got to her teens and realized it wouldn't happen, she began calling our mother by her first name, thinking it would make a point. But she was wrong. Trish dug it. Over the years they had spoken often on the phone, mostly arguing. Debbie was there now, having arrived from San Diego. She was taking a leave of absence from her job as a paralegal. She would stay with Trish till the end.

It was after eleven when I arrived at the apartment. Debbie opened the door and we hugged, then checked each other out. She looked pretty good for a woman with forty in her sights. Still had the freckles, the strawberry blonde hair, the trim body. The only thing different was a little pouch of fat starting under the chin.

"How is she?" I asked.

Debbie took my coat. "Sleeping. Doped up."

I looked around the apartment. Hadn't been there in a long time. The furnishings were strictly Volunteers of America. Trish had never been a good housekeeper. The floors were jammed with piles of magazines, wicker baskets full of yarn, cardboard boxes piled against the walls. I didn't see any dust bunnies, but then Debbie had been there a couple of days already, and she knew how to handle a broom. The place didn't smell very good. A window was slightly open—I could see the curtains rippling in the breeze—but the air stank of medication, cat piss, cigarettes and fried onions. In all my years living with our parents, and then with Trish alone, I don't think I'd ever gone to sleep or awakened in the morning without smelling cigarettes and friend onions. The cat piss was new. When we'd lived in the house on Beecher Street, the cats had gone outside to do their duty.

I put my overnight bag next to the couch I'd be sleeping on. "Maybe I should go in."

"That's probably a good idea. It's a shock, Fin. Better you see her for the first time when she's asleep. You don't do a poker face very well."

I nodded. "So where's Kevin?"

"Supermarket."

I nodded again. "Okay," I said, "here goes."

Very quietly I opened the door to my mother's bedroom and went in. She was curled on her side in the middle of her double bed, under a green and white striped blanket I recognized from the old days. Her nightstand was a shrine to entropy. A tissue box, a small bucket, a water glass, pill bottles, ashtray, pack of cigarettes, other stuff in disarray. I couldn't look at it. Certain types of clutter give me a queasy feeling. The books on the floor looked as if they'd slipped off the bed. I saw the word "Astrology" on one of the covers.

I had expected her to be thinner, and she was. But the thing that tore at me was her face. Even in sleep it was drawn tight. Her breathing was deep and regular, but there was no peace in her expression. Her life had become pain.

I sat in a chair next to the bed and watched her sleep. Trish and I had shared some time on the planet, and now it was almost over. At that moment I didn't feel there was anything to be learned by examining our past. Maybe that would come later, in some kind of afterlife. Maybe there'd be a council of robed elders guiding us through holographic visions that would make us alternately cringe and howl with laughter. But for now I just wanted to let go of all that I felt. It was time to cry. Let it out now while she was asleep. Not that I was ashamed, mind you, I just didn't want to alarm her. She knew she was a goner, so why rub her nose in it with my face all screwed up like a baby's.

I allowed the scalding tears to pour out of my eyes and down my cheeks. After a minute I reached for the tissues and knocked over a medicine bottle, and Trish woke up.

I blew my nose quickly and wadded up the tissue. I wiped the wetness from my face with the sleeve of my flannel shirt. Her eyes were open but not in focus. I waited, thinking she might fall back into her web of sleep.

But she turned her head to me and smiled. "Finny. My god, it's good to see you."

She reached out a bony hand. I leaned forward and took it.

"Hi, Mom." At the moment I didn't trust myself to say anything more.

Her smile grew. The drawn, pained look on her face softened. "Now you're all here," she said. She coughed a little. It wasn't much, but there was a depth to it that frightened me. "Can you prop me up?"

I slid my hand behind her neck and held her forward while I positioned two plump pillows under her head. "How's that?"

"It's good." She hoisted herself up on her elbows, blinked and rubbed her eyes in the dim light and smacked her dry lips together. I was about to freshen her water glass but she said, "Now be a good boy, please, and hand me my cigarettes."

I did what I was told. Why shouldn't she finish the job she'd started on herself with tobacco? Always I had complained about her smoking, and a fat lot of good it had done. So I said nothing. I even lit a match for the cigarette. She had only taken two puffs when the violent coughing began. I watched helplessly as her frail body gave in to the painful spasms, doubling her over and transforming her face into a mask of agony. As the coughs tore through her delicate ribcage, she

292

reached out to me again. I took the cigarette from between her fingers. Her hand dropped to the bed before I could grab hold of it.

I didn't know what to do, but then the door opened and Debbie rushed in and went to the bed. She swore when she smelled the smoke, then took a washcloth from the bucket on the nightstand and gently wiped the phlegm and saliva from our mother's lips and chin. Trish fell back against the pillows, her face wet with perspiration and tears. Each labored breath ended in another brief spasm, but gradually relief came to her.

"Please," said Debbie. "I know it's hard, but try to remember this the next time you feel like smoking."

Trish waved her hand toward the nightstand, a look of resignation on her face. "Throw them out."

Debbie scooped up the cigarettes and shoved them in the pocket of her jeans. She shot me a quick sorrowful glance. "Is there anything I can get you, Mom?" she asked.

Trish just shook her head. Debbie left quietly and closed the door. For a few minutes it was quiet in the room. "Did you catch me on SportsCenter?" I finally asked.

Her eyes were shut, but she smiled a little and nodded her head.

"Not my best moment," I said. I talked some about the year I was having with the Cossacks, gave her a rundown on a few of the more colorful guys on the team. She smiled the whole time I was talking. Then she said, "I need to sleep now, hon."

I got up and leaned over her and put a light kiss on her forehead. "Sleep well," I said. "I'll be on the couch if you need me."

She was asleep even before I had straightened up. If I had said I loved her then, she wouldn't have heard me. But I wouldn't have said it anyway. I loved her, of course, but it wasn't the sort of thing one said in the Connors family, for reasons I still don't fully understand. I thought of Laura, then, who I missed fiercely at that moment, and who said "I love you" to Cody every night when she tucked him in. And Cody said it right back, and never mechanically. You could hear the feeling in it always.

Debbie and I were on the couch catching up on each other's lives and talking about the situation at hand when Kevin returned from the supermarket with two plastic bags of groceries hanging from his fists. "Hey," he said, when he saw me. "How was the trip, Chip?"

"It was alright, Dwight," I said. This was automatic, after years of programming, first from our dad, and then from each other. Dad loved a quick rhyme. Often when we were young he would be the one making breakfast while Trish nursed a booze or drug hangover. Not that Dad hadn't indulged as well, but his powers of recuperation were stronger. Proud of his way with a fried egg over medium, confident that his home fries with chopped scallions and paprika were culinary miracles, he would ask us kids, as we dug in, something on the order of, "How's the food, dude?" I clearly remember it was Kevin who first rose to the challenge, answering, "Not bad, Dad." After a few weeks of exhausting the finite possibilities of this banter (How's the spaghetti, Freddy? But you soon ran out of foodstuffs to rhyme with), we branched out into non-food-related areas. If a hipster could say, "See you later, alligator," our dad could certainly say, "Take a walk, chalk," when he wanted you out of the room. But just as hipster number two had the responsibility to keep things reptilian with "After awhile, crocodile," you would have to put a writing instrument into your reply: "See you then, pen."

Trish considered it a strain to produce rhymes on demand. One time she served us French fries she'd baked on a cookie tin. With a sly smile, Trish asked, "How are the fries, guys?"

"Delish, Trish," I said. My response was so immediate (I'd been saving it up), that it unnerved her, and she never tried it again.

Now I followed my brother into the kitchen and leaned against the counter while he put milk and cold cuts into the refrigerator. "I have two beds in my room at Day's Inn," said Kevin. "You're welcome to one. That couch doesn't look real comfortable."

It was a nice offer, but I'm a lot hardier than Kevin. "I'm only staying the one night," I said, "so I guess it'll be here."

Kevin nodded. "I'm leaving tomorrow, too."

Debbie came out for a soda and the three of us stood under the bright fluorescent light, saying nothing, just feeling the sad strangeness of the moment. "Know what?" said Debbie. "This is probably the last time we'll ever be in the same room together. I mean, you're not coming back for the funeral, right, Kev?"

She said it matter-of-factly, but with an undertone of disapproval. Kevin ignored the undertone. "Right you are, sis."

"That's assuming a lot," I said. "You really don't think we'll hook up again?"

Debbie poured her cream soda into a glass and dropped the empty plastic bottle into a paper bag on the floor filled with other plastic bottles destined for recycling. She took a sip and smacked her lips appreciatively. "Let's be honest," she said. "Our family didn't come with the right kind of glue. We won't stick together. That's just how it is."

She walked breezily out of the kitchen. Kevin and I looked at each other in silence, like a couple of kids told to keep their mouths shut and not leave the room until they were sent for. "You want a beer?" I asked.

"More than ever."

I opened the fridge and extracted a bottle of Moosehead Ale. I would not be having one myself, but I enjoyed the cold wet feel of the bottle against the palm of my hand. I could at least partake of this small, satisfying ritual—

handing a beer to my brother across the space of a searingly bright kitchen.

The sound of a laugh track lured us into the living room. Debbie was at one end of the couch, remote in hand, staring with blank eyes at a sitcom. I sat down beside her. Kevin plopped down next to me. We watched TV for a while, making well-placed, acid comments about the crap in front of us, some show about a wisecracking family of five (two teens, middle-aged mom and dad, crusty live-in uncle) who were pawns of the sexual impulse. I couldn't take it anymore. I snatched the remote from Debbie and flicked around, finally settling on *The Honeymooners*. "We're in luck," I said. It was the episode where Ralph's mother-in-law spills the beans about a Broadway whodunit, and Ralph roars in her face, "YOU, ARE A *BLABBERMOUTH!*" and all hell breaks loose. I love this episode except for the ending, which always gives me a pang. Here's a guy, big and fat, no money in his pocket, self-centered and verbally abusive, and yet his pretty wife always forgives him. Why couldn't all husbands and wives love each other like Ralph and Alice and make up no matter what? When I was younger, I used to ask myself why our own parents couldn't have held it together like people on TV. I never voiced this, because Kevin or Debbie would have said, "It's a TV show, ya dope." And they would have been right.

So we sat there and laughed and felt warm and sad with the Kramdens, and then I lost myself in memories of growing up, and how strongly I had wished things to be different.

There was a story our father used to tell. One day when I was three or four I went with Dad to the post office. It was Christmas season and the place was jammed with people lined up to send packages. I wandered off and lost sight of my father, and started bawling. Dad simply walked the few steps to where I was standing in the forest of legs and took my hand. I stopped crying the moment I grabbed his hand, Dad would say. I had been lost, and now found, was happy. My father often repeated this story in my presence, and I knew he wanted me to believe that no matter how lost I might become, he would always appear to take my hand. This was before his drinking grew out of control, before he left. What it taught me to believe is that words of kindly intent are like the fragrances coming from a field of flowers on a windy day. You take them in and they fill you with wonder and joy, and then the wind shifts and they vanish.

We beat Albany as expected and began preparing for the big game against Manchester. We had more than a week to get ready because the game was scheduled for a Sunday—the one Sunday of the season when no NFL teams were engaged—the Sunday preceding the Super Bowl. We were psyched. Even the national media were getting interested. The game would fill the terrible void of a weekend with no NFL football. ESPN cut a deal with FOX and borrowed Madden and Summerall to do the broadcast. It was great to be getting all this attention.

The Giants had made it to the Super Bowl that year, and this increased my pleasure because I've been a Giant fan all my life. I'm a Giant fan because I was raised in the state of New York, closer to the Big Apple than to Buffalo. Your region is in your blood, I believe, and you should follow your home-turf teams, which is why I have contempt for

Cowboy fans from the Northeast. America's team my ass. You shouldn't be a Cowboy fan unless you can look out your window and see armadillos running around.

Lou was after us to do our jobs. Keep training, keep practicing, pay attention at meetings. Study the game plan. And stay out of trouble.

I put in a lot of time on the treadmill, often next to Bobby Hertzig, who ran for conditioning more than anyone else on the team and drowned out the hollering and clanging of the weight room with headphones over his ears and a Judy Garland CD spinning in his Discman. Camaraderie was high. We all wanted the same thing.

I spent Christmas and New Year's with Laura and Cody. I was getting sucked in and felt glad about it. Trish was still on the planet. Kevin was gone, but Debbie would stay till the end. I was fit and uninjured. I was ready for the Northeastern Football League's Championship game, or whatever else might come my way.

The Cossacks and the Manchester Purple Demons had identical won-lost records, but since Manchester had won the only head-to-head competition, they were the home team. We didn't care. We would have played them in a parking lot in Reykjavic.

One thing that annoyed me was the preponderance of newsprint devoted to the Purple Demons. I guess the scribes thought they were more interesting. They liked Manchester's head coach, a fifty-year-old black man named Arthur Hynes. Tall and grim-faced, with a get-it-done air about him, he reminded people of Morgan Freeman as the President in that movie about the runaway asteroid. Hynes had come from South Carolina for a term at Fort Dix, then enrolled in Rutgers as a twenty-five year-old freshman where he played halfback for three years, earning All-American honorable mention. A knee injury in the Senior bowl destroyed his hopes of playing in the NFL, but he went into coaching and distinguished himself at every level. Before taking the job with Manchester, he spent four years building an excellent special teams unit for the New England Patriots. His wife was a school principal and their house in Methuen trembled with the shouts and laughter of their brood of six, including two adopted Korean orphans. Arthur Hynes led by example, running laps and bench-pressing three-hundred pounds every morning before breakfast. His hobbies were gourmet cooking, raising iguanas, and reading military history. He was great copy.

Sports Illustrated did a profile on Arthur Hynes. ESPN ran a segment on Antonio Sciacca, Manchester's Sicilian import, a behemoth who'd been discovered at a *Strongest Man* competition, and who ate his fusilli and meatballs from a mixing bowl. And Bob Ryan of the Boston Globe wrote a story about Stooge Flynn, in which it was revealed that Flynn collected serial killer action figures. This was news to me; I hadn't known that such "toys" existed. An accompanying photo showed Flynn, looking very Larry-like in casual clothes, posed next to a shelf holding plastic simulacra of Jack the Ripper, Ted Bundy, and John Wayne Gacey. (Gacey, Ryan commented, looked disturbingly like Mike Ditka.)

We were not ignored altogether, but as the Frank DeFords and Tony Kornheisers of the press were busy covering the Super Bowl, the Cossacks got Mike Danvers, a benchwarmer who wrote sports for the New York Post. By his own admission, Danvers occasionally couldn't even get his stories into print. He took Lou and me to a fancy burger joint, the kind of place that has old newspaper headlines shellacked on wooden planks stuck to the walls, and faux Tiffany lamps hanging so low over the tables that they made your scalp sweat. Danvers was a big guy with the flushed face and wide waist of a heavy drinker. His hair was reddish-brown and he had a bristly mustache and dark laughing eyes. There was a hint of charm about him—he was gregarious and commanding—but after his third luncheon martini, personality defects began to show themselves like dead fish bobbing at the surface of a pond. He took a disparaging tone regarding the legitimacy of the NFA, and began boasting of his own exploits and achievements, such as they were. I mentioned the amusing article about Stooge Flynn, and Danvers responded by calling Bob Ryan a punk. Said he had floored him with a karate kick to the chest one besotted night during the Final Four.

"For God's sake, why?" asked Lou.

"Disagreement over a broad," said Danvers, hurling himself at the bowl of New England clam chowder the waitress set before him. He had the table manners of a gulag survivor, attacking the chowder with slurps and gasps and spattering a portion of it on his chin and necktie. I watched in astonishment as Danvers somehow got an oyster cracker stuck up his nose. I don't know what disgusted me more, the little splash the cracker made when he expelled it from his nostril, or the fact that the same cracker ended up in the next spoonful he greedily brought to his lips. Right about then, Bobby Hertzig and DeCurtis Johnson sauntered into the place and joined the table before I could warn them away. When Bobby found out Danvers was from the Post, he zeroed in. "You've been in the Giant locker room," he said. "Please tell me Jason Sehorn is gay. Tell me he is even if he isn't. God, what a hunk! I call him Jason Sehorney. I see him and I get horny."

Danvers tore a roll in half and slathered it with butter, getting his fingers greasy. "Sorry," he said, shaking his head. "You're peelin' the wrong banana with that one."

Bobby gave a little cry of disappointment.

"But listen here," continued Danvers. He leaned forward conspiratorially. "You wanna know who's queer as tits on a bull?"

"Sure," I said. "Give us the scoop."

In a stage whisper that blew his boozy breath into our faces, Danvers named the eminent former head coach and general manager. Bobby and DeCurtis both laughed out loud.

"Oh ye of little faith," said Danvers, his mouth working at the buttered roll. "Ask yourself this, bright boys. How come he keeps leaving these great jobs? How come he leaves everyone in the lurch all of a sudden?" Elbows on the table, hands joined and one quivering index sticking out at us, he said, "I'll tell you why. He can't stand to be in the locker room. It tortures him. And then when he quits he can't wait to get back."

Later that day Lou put in a call to the Post and got the goods on Mike Danvers. He was not employed by the paper, and only rarely was given some work as a stringer. A former sportswriter for various small town papers, he had boozed his way out of every job and now supported himself by writing pseudonymous narratives for bondage magazines. Once in awhile he might throw a drunken haymaker at someone, but the Bob Ryan story was false. He would, Lou's contact suggested, probably end up in a rubber room someday.

Kickoff was four p.m. The snow started a little past noon. Flurries first, then the wind gusting and the snow swirling so thick you'd go dizzy watching it. Manchester was caught in the teeth of a major snowstorm, and everyone loved it. You knew that John Madden would be up in the booth saying how great it was that the teams were fighting it out in a big ol' blizzard. The stadium was packed. People had snow in their hair and eyebrows and drank hard liquor from flasks. A fair number of those in attendance had come from Centerport. Already a few fights had broken out, but the local police and a rented crew of security guards were keeping the general order. But they had trouble stopping the snowballs, which streamed through the air like antiaircraft fire during a blitz. It promised to be the most fun day this bleak New Hampshire town had ever seen.

We were noisy and antsy in the locker room, eager to get out in the driving snow and kick some ass. An official came in and gave us the word. Ten minutes to kickoff. Lou had everyone gather round.

"Gentlemen," he began, "football is a woman."

He stopped, savoring a silence broken only by random coughs and the crepitations of men shifting their weight in full uniform and cleats. In the little area at the center of the room he slowly paced.

"But football isn't just any woman. Football is a young virgin with the face of an angel and the bosoms of a lap-dancer. The first time you laid eyes on her you fell in love. She was a few rows ahead of you in study hall, and you stared at the nape of her neck, noticing how it looked like cream underneath the curl of her honey blond hair. Her ankles were crossed, and you daydreamed of touching the backs of her perfect legs."

There was more coughing, some shuffling of feet, but we all stared at Lou, listening hard. What the hell was he talking about?

"My boys, that first glimpse of such heartbreaking beauty was your first training camp.

Your first encounter with the Goddess Football."

He stopped again, surveying the rapt, staring faces. "Do you understand what I'm telling you? Football is the eternal feminine. Football pulls you forward against your will. You are powerless to resist."

He resumed his pacing. "So what did you do next? You asked her out on a date, that's what you did. And that was your first taste of her, your first game. Then you had more dates. More games. You were drawn closer, and with each step a little more of your own will was imposed on this lovely, vibrant, sensuous female creature who desired you but needed to be tamed, dominated. So you dominated—you won—and these were your hand jobs, and they felt wonderful."

Now there was laughter. But it was brief. We were waiting to hear what came next.

"Then you realized you wanted more. A lot more. So what happened? You had setbacks. Problems. Your car wouldn't start when you were supposed to pick her up on a date. Her scowling father met you at the door and you could tell he had you pegged for a budding rapist. You took her to a diner and she kept glancing at a cute guy in the next booth. Lads, these were your fumbles, your injuries, your losses. But all they made you do was try harder. *Never give up* became your mantra. And now, because you never gave up, because you continued to work and struggle and sweat, it's time for the payoff. It's time to cash in."

Lou stood like a statue now, his fists clenched in front of his chest. "O my brothers in sport, my seekers at the gate of joy! That young virgin with big bosoms is lying naked on her bed. Her legs are open, her arms outstretched, her eyes misty with longing. You have waited for this moment all your lives. Each one of you is a colossus of manhood, throbbing with erectile savagery! What will you do? Will you shrink back, afraid that you're not man enough to take the prize offered to you? Will fear and hesitation destroy you at the very moment of triumph? Or will you be men, *strong* men, and plunge powerfully into the pulsating paradise of victory? What is it, Cossacks? Fear? Or victory?"

Lou's voice had become a roar. His fists rose in front of his face, and the veins in his neck stood out like steel cords.

310

A chorus of voices cried, "Victory!" At the same moment I distinctly heard one or two confused but exuberant souls yell, "Pussy!"

And we were off. We burst out of the locker room and took the field like a conquering horde. Luther Moffitt was at the head of the pack, screaming at the top of his lungs, *"Fuck the virgin! Fuck the virgin!"* You should have seen the looks on the faces of the Purple Demons when they heard this very unusual war cry.

We won the toss and elected to defend the north goal, a strategic move designed to put Manchester at an immediate disadvantage. Their quarterback would have the icy wind knifing at his face. Their wideouts would be running into a gale, a force field pushing them back, and the passes thrown their way would wobble and dip in the driving storm. They would have to punt, and the ball would feel like a brick on the punter's foot, and it would sail maybe fifteen yards and give us killer field position. It was a fine plan, but it didn't work.

With the wind at his back, Reg Hastings boomed the kickoff high and long. Cold air takes a lot out of a kick, but Hastings really got his foot into it, and Octavius Dee caught the ball four yards deep in the end zone. On a field slick with snow, and with a punishing wind in his face, Octavius Dee was expected by all to do the prudent thing: take a knee and let his offense start from the 20. But that's the beauty of football—people don't always do the expected, especially under pressure. Dee ran out of the end zone past his astonished blocker (who had motioned for him to down the ball), and headed for the center of the field. It looked like a charging Carthage Lee would nail him at the 12, but Lee slipped in the snow, and then Guy Smeeks tripped over Lee's fallen body, and Octavius Dee found a crack in the wedge. He squirted through it and angled toward the sideline, with only Reg Hastings to beat.

Hastings was a strapping fellow, a fine athlete with good speed. He often spoke of his days playing soccer and rugby at Loughboro University. He had a 210-pound hardbody and in practice would run into larger men without fear. I once played tennis against him and marveled at his quickness. As I watched from the sidelines, I thought maybe the Brit had a chance of stopping Octavius Dee. Later

I would recall a spirited late-night conversation when DeCurtis Johnson had patiently tried to explain to Hastings the politically incorrect truth that the American Negro athlete, a product of specialized breeding in a Darwinian crucible of adversity, could punch harder, jump higher, and run faster than the majority of Caucasian athletes from America or any other country. Hastings wasn't having it, and he thought even more ludicrous the theory of Kenny Liebowitz, who inserted his two cents to the effect that Blacks were true earthlings, and whites were the descendants of crash-landed aliens from another world. "You got that from the *Twilight Zone,*" said Ipana Brown, the fourth member of this particular panel discussion. "Besides, if y'all are from outer space, then how come you ain't got super powers, like Superman?"

Now the events on the field favored DeCurtis Johnson's side of the debate. Hastings proved a step too slow, and Octavius Dee turned the corner and ran unmolested to the end zone. And just like that it was 6-0.

Manchester made the extra point. Then their kickoff went out of bounds, a penalty that gave us the ball on the 40. After a three-yard stumble forward by Charley Hooks, Drew Danielson threw a couple of wild passes, and it was time to punt, and so began two quarters of error-filled, weather-beaten, defensive football.

Real football fans, and the players on the field, knew that this was a pretty goddamn good game despite the miscues and slipping and sliding. Pinpoint passing, crisply-run routes, and startling, break-away runs seldom occur on a field of snow and ice. A halfback might spurt through the line and make people miss and appear to be off to the races, but then he'll lose his footing and slide on his chest for a nine-yard pickup before a pursuing defensive tackle pancakes him. A wideout might manage to juke his way to an open space while the defender skids on the ice with wind-milling arms, but the quarterback's frozen fingers will betray him, and the pass will fall short. In such conditions you play for field position, and you hold on to the football like it's your first born, and you wait to capitalize on the other team's fumble or tipped pass.

At the start of the second quarter, Manchester fair-caught a punt at their own 38 and commenced a drive to our 17, where they stalled and had to settle for a field goal. Just before the half they were driving again, but Phillip Woo made a pretty one-handed swipe of a wobbly pass and began a sixty-yard run down the sideline. The way was clear to the end zone, and Woo would have made it easily if not for the bumbling intervention of Taters Delevan. Even though he wasn't needed, Taters did the proper thing and ran alongside Woo, turning his head and lifting his elbows up in a challenge to any would-be tacklers. There was no one within twenty yards of Woo, but Taters Delevan was determined to be a one-man convoy. Alas, he drifted too close to Woo, and his large bottom bumped the 178-pound cornerback out of bounds on the 12. We couldn't punch it in from there, and after a field goal by Hastings, we were down 10-3 as the gun sounded the end of the first half.

An odd thing happened to me during half-time. The locker room was noisy and busy, as expected, with players having their bumps and bruises tended to and coaches running around making adjustments and shouting encouragement. I had been in the game for five plays. On one, I made a nice block on a cornerback allowing Dunnan Bradstreet to pick up an extra five yards. On another play, I ran a decoy fly pattern and lost my footing and wiped out. So I was wet and cold and a little muddy. And for the first time in my life as a player, it bothered me.

I sat by myself on a bench pondering this curious development. I had always been the type who would play touch football in the street with the neighborhood kids, or run pass patterns in a field at dusk after an all-day soaking rain and end up covered head-to-toe in mud. I would do these things simply because I loved the game. So what the hell was this? There were still thirty minutes of football to play in the biggest game of my life, and I was thinking I'd rather be in dry socks and a warm bathrobe watching it on TV.

Ray Whipple sat down next to me in his clean dry uniform and started chatting me up. His ribs were okay and he'd been given the go-ahead, but hadn't played yet. I nodded along with everything Ray said, even huffed and hollered a little, but my heart wasn't in it.

But I knew this might be my last game, and when I went back out on the field I was ready. Whatever I had felt while sitting soaked and shivering on that bench was pushed into the back of my brain. I wanted to catch a pass. I wanted to hit somebody. I wanted to embody the phrase a former teammate had once shouted in practice, a phrase the teammate had learned in the humid hell of Marine boot camp: *Positive Mental Sickness.*

The fourth quarter began with the score tied at 10. Both defenses hunkered down. Twice the teams traded punts. Everyone played conservatively. You didn't want to be the guy who lunged for an interception only to have the ball sail beyond your outstretched fingers and into the big hands of a split end on his way downfield for the winning score. You didn't want to be the punt returner with moves so flashy that you faked the ball right out of your own hands. You could sense the tightness in the air. You knew it would take some loosey-goosey son of a bitch to put the game away.

Who else, but Placebo Washington?

317

For half the season Placebo had been hearing himself compared to Randy Moss, and now he wanted to bring the hammer down and show the world it was Moss that should be compared to him.

The scoreboard clock showed 2:48. We had the ball on our own 37. After a brief respite, the wind and snow had gathered force again, and was blowing hard in our faces. I ran onto the field with a play from Lou, a buttonhook-and-go to Washington. When I got to the huddle I heard angry voices and confusion. Placebo was complaining that he was open all the damn time. Ray was insisting that he could beat the linebacker on a screen pass. Various linemen were mumbling that they could blow a hole in the defense for whoever might feel like running to daylight. And Drew was telling everyone to shut the fuck up. Nearly breathless, I announced Lou's play. In the sharp tones of a drill sergeant, Drew made sure everyone knew their assignments.

We lined up at the 37, nose-to-nose with the crouching Purple Demons. Drew Barked the signals. From Manchester's side of the line, somebody snarled, "I'm gonna knock you out, whore-beater." Drew paid no mind. Neal Zank snapped the ball into his hands, and Drew turned and faked a handoff to Charley Hooks. Hooks picked up a blitzing linebacker, and Drew stood tall and strong in the pocket.

Placebo ran the buttonhook to perfection, sprinting nine yards straight ahead and then turning and stopping abruptly for the pass.

Except there was no pass.

Drew snapped his arm forward but didn't let go of the ball. But the cornerback had committed himself and lurched forward, and the pump-fake froze the safety who was lingering behind Placebo, providing backup. At that moment Placebo turned up field and blew past both defenders.

Drew let it fly just as he was hit by Stooge Flynn, the second man coming in on a blitz. Flynn spat and growled curses at Danielson as he drove him into the ground, but the ball was already on its way. It was a pretty pass, a tight spiral high in the air, catching the gleam of the lights as it soared through the blizzard. Had the wind been at Drew's back, Placebo could have kept his stride and caught the ball out in front of him and loped into the end zone. But the wind held it up, and Placebo stopped to make the grab, and he was tackled on the 11 by a trailing safety.

Manchester dug in. On first down Drew rolled to his right and zipped a bullet to James Veltry that bounced and skidded on the snowy turf. On second down Drew tried another pass—this one to Berenyi over the middle. The Mancunian cornerback batted it away at the last moment. On third down Drew dropped back to pass and was flattened by the Stooge again, a loss of seven yards. But we were still in field goal range.

The snowy field presented a problem. Hastings needed a clear alley from the spot where he would plant his foot, to the point where Drew would hold the ball for him to kick. Some of the Cossacks were bending over to try and wipe away the snow. The forty-second clock was running out. Drew yelled for Chunky Hanrahan to drop his fat ass on the ground. The 315-pound guard complied, and Drew and Klaus Kohler took hold of his legs and used his big butt as a snow plow. It worked; the alley for Hastings to two-step into the kick was all clear.

Hastings booted the ball through the middle of the uprights, and we were on the brink of winning the whole shebang with under two minutes to play.

"Hold the motherfuckers! Hold 'em!" yelled Ipana Brown from the sidelines as our special teams lined up to kick off. Hastings drove the ball perfectly. Not so far that the returner could build up a head of steam, and not so short that they'd get the ball near midfield. It dropped at the 13, and their return man was lucky to pick it up and carry it six yards to the 19.

Manchester lined up on offense. I looked at the clock. 1:44. I knew that anything over a minute was sufficient time for them to move the ball close enough for a field goal, but I still liked our chances. The Purple Demons had only one timeout remaining, and now the wind was crazier than ever, swirling in all directions at once.

On the sidelines, we had our guts in a boil. Next to me stood Charley Hooks, jumping straight up and down like a maniac. On the other side of me Elwood Pye was speaking gibberish to himself. All we could do was stand there helplessly, praying that the defense would hang tough.

But on the first play, it looked like the defense was ready to fold.

I have always hated the prevent defense. I know it's a sound, logical way to keep the big play from happening, but I also know what it does to defensive players. It fosters an attitude of containment instead of rapine and destruction, which is what every defensive player must have in order to do his job. Now I watched in horror as on the first play the slackened defense allowed split end Alton Wingate to catch a pass over the middle—against coverage so soft it put one in mind of bunny rabbits and eiderdown—and run and slide twenty-seven yards before being stopped at the 46. The play consumed a mere 12 seconds off the clock, and now Manchester was at midfield.

"Oh, fuck me. Fuck me." This helpless cry came from Tom Patterson, standing a few feet away from me. It meant trouble, since Patterson was the defensive backs coach.

But the defense buckled down. Manchester tried a draw, not a bad risk, since everyone in the stadium figured pass. But Joe

Mankowski tripped up the ball carrier after seven yards. Quarterback Greg Lawson, a little guy who could scramble and throw short passes, hit fullback Hogarth Van Gelder with a screen pass for another five that picked up the first down. Now they had the ball at our 38. Fifteen more yards and they'd be in field goal range. The clock was down to forty-six seconds, enough time, I knew, for Manchester to get the job done.

And it happened on the very next play.

Lawson took the snap and dropped back to pass. With ease, he eluded the first Cossack to break through the line and stepped into a moving pocket to survey the field. What he saw was the same thing that I and everyone else in the stadium saw at the same time.

Alton Wingate had broken free over the middle, somehow finding an open space in the mass of converging bodies. It was a good chance for a completion, as Joe Mankowski would need at least four or five running steps to close the gap. It might very well be the completed pass that would put them in field goal range. I watched in anguish as Lawson cocked his arm for the pass.

But then it got worse.

As Mankowski closed, as the ball left Lawson's hand, as every spectator in the stands, on the sidelines, and at home in front of the tube held their breaths, Luther Moffitt came from out of nowhere and torpedoed himself at Wingate's midsection.

He missed.

The ball sunk into Wingate's hands, and Moffitt's barreling body flew past and rammed into the chest of Joe Mankowski, knocking the wind out of it. The two linebackers lay twitching in the snow, and Wingate, astonished at his luck, ran down the middle of the field toward pay dirt.

I let out a howl of torment, a howl lost in the wind and the cries of my teammates. The game was over.

I watched with a sinking, sickish feeling as Wingate ran to the end zone, prancing all alone at the 20, already holding the ball high in the air to taunt and celebrate. At the 10, Wingate slowed down and went into a Groucho walk, still brandishing the ball over his head. Gemini Harper came up from the rear, but would not get there in time. I knew Wingate would score easily, in a matter of seconds.

I was mistaken.

Somebody in the stands threw a snow-ball. Now, snowballs had been flying around for the whole game. But not too many had reached the benches or the field. This one came from the end zone seats, however, and the person who flung it had a strong arm and lucky aim. It hit Alton Wingate's hand, and the ball came loose.

Wingate was moving forward, but now the ball was bouncing across the icy turf in the opposite direction. There was a moment of utter, eerie silence, as if the breath had been knocked out of every fan in the stadium. It was like the two or three seconds between a toddler's fall to the pavement and the howl of shock and pain that bursts out of him. And then a cry arose from the stadium unlike any I had ever heard. It was high-pitched, a shriek, a screaming like something out of a slaughterhouse. The ball was wobbling to a stop, and Wingate had hit the brakes and fallen backwards, one hand propped on the field. He turned his head to face the ball and scuttered his feet in the snow like a cartoon character trying to get purchase. Gemini Harper had seen the ball come loose and was bearing down on it, his arms reaching forward in a predatory lurch. The stadium trembled with the seismic thunder of jumping feet, boomed with the roar of the frustrated thousands who could not at that instant clasp the ball to their bosoms. Harper and Wingate reached the ball at the same time, their hands clawing, their helmets ramming. Then the others came, and the ball was lost under a pile of players who kicked and fought like dying prey in the jaws of a lion, and it was the beginning of pandemonium.

I wanted to run out on the field and so did everyone else on the sideline, but we knew better. We pressed as far over the line as we dared, shouting and waving our fists. Lou stared with demon eyes at the pile up, his arms outstretched to hold his children back from the fray. The refs fought to untangle the cluster of pumping thick limbs and bull necks. One by one, players were pulled away as the refs dug deeper into the pile, some burrowing from the top, others close to the ground, straining to see.

And then it came. The signal.

The field judge rose to his full height, and with the power of total authority, he turned away from the goal line and pointed down the field. Fumble. Centerport ball.

In the chaos that followed—fistfights in the stands, a meteor storm of snowballs, the Manchester coaches foaming at the mouth, our own coaches clapping and hollering support for the decision—the refs conferred among themselves while the field judge watched the replay, remaining under the protective shroud for a long time, heedless of the snowballs exploding at his feet. He emerged with a face of stone, pressed the button at his belt to activate his field microphone. "After the replay, the ruling on the field stands. Manchester fumble, recovered by Centerport. Centerport ball on the 14."

More chaos, more fights, more screaming. But things settled down. I stood on the sidelines with a dazed grin on my face, jostled by the hurly-burly all around me. Play resumed. Drew Danielson took three knees, and that was it.

Game over.

Manchester protested the game, of course. There was a near-riot in the stands, and they almost killed the poor idiot who'd thrown the snowball, even though it turned out he was a Purple Demon fan too drunk to know what he was doing. All agreed that the officials were lucky to escape with their testicles. Their real thrashing came in the media, at the hands of columnists, letter writers, and talk-radio bully-boys. Many suggested that the zebras were guilty of having a racist response to a situation—the taunting and dancing of a Black man—perceived by White America as a threat. It didn't seem to matter that one of the referees was an African American; they called him an Uncle Tom. DeCurtis Johnson is currently writing an op-ed piece on all of this. I believe he will do a fine job.

Cody couldn't wait to talk to me about the game. He's grown into quite the football fan. When I came to the house, Cody dragged me to the computer to show me the million or so articles about the game on the Internet. I found this astonishing. I'm old enough to re-member when you had to hoof it down to the library and ask for spools of...what did they call it? Oh yes, *microfiche.* Now you could sit like a lump in your room and turn on your computer and all of a sudden you're a scholar.

Well, I said, to anyone who would listen, they could discuss the controversy until the sun exploded, but they couldn't change the fact that the Cossacks had won. I still had my unwashed jersey, stinking of dried champagne, to prove it. And I had a tape of the locker room celebration, too, courtesy of Laura, who taped it for me off the TV. My favorite moment was when somebody shoved a microphone at Kilmer Joyce and asked him what he was going to do now. I knew the person expected a variation of the standard "I'm going to Disney World" response. But Kilmer Joyce, wearing the smile of a man in rapture, said, "I jus' gonna walk around grinnin' like a possum eatin' shit from a silver spoon."

I'd say that's how we all felt.

The night before the Super Bowl—the *real* Super Bowl, the one in Phoenix between the Giants and the Raiders—Teddy Mankopf threw a big shindig for the Cossacks at the Centerport Country Club. I wanted to bring Laura, but she had stomach flu and wasn't going anywhere. It was a disappointment for both of us.

"I won't go," I said. "Hell, I'm not into parties and drinking anyway, you know that. I'd rather stay here with you."

Laura's stomach hurt from vomiting. She was walking funny—when she walked at all—because her rectum was sore from repeated discharges of diarrhea. This was not information she had shared with me, but I was able to figure it out. She was too weak to shower, and kept her bathrobe cinched tight so her body odor would not waft into my breathing space. She hated the way her hair looked, all tangled and dirty.

"Okay," she said, "stay here and miss the party. You can walk me to the bathroom every forty minutes. It'll be fun."

I saw her point. Missing the victory party would be a terrible mistake. And being no saint, I might even hold it against her in some crabbed little part of my guy-brain.

So I went. And I had a swell time, drinking sodas and watching most of my teammates get drunk. They had a local band good at covering old Cream and Hendrix. There was dancing, but I stood on the periphery, gabbing and laughing and enjoying the hors d'oeuvres.

Amid all the merriment, Lou came up to me with a serious look on his face. "Did you hear what happened today?"

I shook my head.

"It's Scotty Kay," said Lou. "Blew his brains out this morning."

Well, I thought, Scotty Kay wasn't someone I'd known personally. I wouldn't let it ruin my night. Scotty Kay was a man everyone figured would not be getting his life back anywhere close to where it had once been. There was a tragic inevitability, a certainty of decline about him. But you also hoped that since he'd made it this far, after all the humiliation, he would at least keep trying, maybe find a woman and a job and a quiet life for himself. I have great sympathy for suicides, and for those left behind in the wake of self-murder. It is my opinion that my father had committed slow suicide every time he polished off another twelve-pack of Old Milwaukee. If I kept thinking about this, it *would* ruin my night.

"What a drag," I said.

"Eloquently put," said Lou. "You know what he did?"

"Tell me."

"He drove south all night till he found a lake that wasn't frozen over. Woke up some guy had a place that rented canoes. Paddled out to the center of the lake, took a .38 out of his pocket and put it in his mouth and pulled the trigger."

"Christ."

"They found a note in his car. It said he'd thought about the right way of doing this. In a canoe the blast would propel him over the side, and even if the shot didn't kill him, he would drown. And there would be no mess to clean up. No trouble for anyone else."

We stood for a minute without talking. Then Lou said, "On a happier note, I must tell you I got a call last week from Ernie Accorsi. They may have a spot for me on the coaching staff."

I knew Ernie Accorsi was the general manager for the New York Giants, and that he and Lou had been acquainted for years. I was happy for Lou, and I said so, trying to mask my instant concern for my own future. I'd been hoping for another year, perhaps, with the Cossacks. If a new coach came in, what then?

Lou sensed the fear behind my smile. "Don't worry, Fin. You did a great job for us this year. If I can swing it, you'll come with me. If not, something else will open up. I'll go to bat for you."

I knew it was a stretch that I would be going to the Giants on Lou's coattails, but I also knew Lou would definitely make good on his promise to help me find a job somewhere. Maybe as an NFL scout. Hell, maybe it *would* even be with the Giants, you never knew.

Lou was a great guy. A true friend. But I had to do what I did next. I couldn't help it.

The band broke into a kick-ass cover of "Born to Be Wild." Lou and I listened and grooved for a bit. Then I leaned close to Lou and shouted into his ear.

"What?" said Lou. The music was very loud.

I pointed down at Lou's feet. He was wearing a pair of Italian loafers. Fairly stylish, actually, but I didn't care. They were perhaps too casual-looking. Borderline slippers or driving shoes. That would be the weakness, the point of attack. Lou's eyes followed my pointing finger.

"Mistake," I yelled, slowly shaking my head. "For God's sake, Lou, don't wear those when you interview with the Giants."

I timed it perfectly. When Lou looked up, I was already gone, slipping away through the crowd. I didn't look back. Imagining the expression on Lou's face was better than seeing it. Laughing, I made for the door, patting backs and shaking hands on the way.

Out in the cold night, I thought of the warm house and the sleeping child and the good woman awaiting me. I imagined Laura frowning on the sofa, half-asleep in the darkness, barely focused on an old movie. I knew she would be glad I had left the party so early, had come back to a woman who was sour and sickly.

The mournful cry of a train whistle pierced the night. It was a sound that always put me in a sad mood, made me think of endless journeys to nowhere. Now it just made me walk faster to my car, to the happiness within my reach.